nothing more
than murder

Other titles available in Vintage Crime/Black Lizard

By Jim Thompson

After Dark, My Sweet
The Getaway
The Grifters
A Hell of a Woman
The Killer Inside Me

By Charles Willeford

The Burnt Orange Heresy
Cockfighter
Pick-Up

By David Goodis

Black Friday
The Burglar
Nightfall
Shoot the Piano Player
Street of No Return

By Charles Williams

The Hot Spot

By Fredric Brown

The Far Cry
His Name Was Death

By Richard Neely

The Plastic Nightmare

nothing more
than murder

jim thompson

VINTAGE CRIME / **BLACK LIZARD**

vintage books • a division of random house, inc. • new york

First Vintage Crime/Black Lizard Edition, March 1991

ISBN 0-679-73309-4
Library of Congress Catalog Card Number: 90-50630

Manufactured in the United States of America
10 9 8 7 6 5 4 3 2 1

nothing more
than murder

1

WANTED: *Unencumbered woman for general
work in out-of-town home. Forty to forty-five;
able to wear size 14 uniform. Excellent wages,
hours. Box No. —*

"I'll let you write in the box number," I told the girl
behind the counter. "Have to let you do something to
earn your money."

She smiled, kind of like an elevator boy smiles when
you ask him if he has lots of ups and downs. "Yes, sir.
What is your name, please?"

"Well," I said, "I'm going to pay for the ad now."

"Yes, sir," she said, just as much as to say you're
damned right you're going to pay now. "We have to
have your name and address, sir."

I told her I was placing the ad for a friend, "Mrs. J.J.
Williamson, room four-nineteen, Crystal Arms Hotel,"
and she wrote it down on a printed slip of paper and
stabbed it over a spike with a lot of others.

"That runs one word over three lines. If you like, I
think I can eliminate a—"

"I want it printed like it stands," I said. "How
much?"

"For three days it will be two dollars and forty-four
cents."

I had a dollar and ninety-six cents in my overcoat pocket—exactly enough if Elizabeth had figured things right. I pulled it out and laid it on the counter, and fumbled around in my pants pocket for some change.

I found a quarter, two nickels, and a few pennies. I dropped them into my coat as soon as I saw they weren't enough, and reached again. The girl stared at my hands—the gloves—her eyebrows up a little.

I came out with a half dollar and slid it across to her. "There," I said, "that makes it."

"Just a minute, sir. You have two cents change coming."

I waved my hand at her to keep it. I didn't want to try to pick up those pennies with my gloves on, and something told me she'd make me pick them up. I wanted to get out of there.

She hollered something just as the door closed, but I didn't turn around. I hit the street and I kept right on walking without looking back.

I guess I must have gone a dozen blocks, just walking along blind, before I realized I was being a chump. I stopped and lighted a cigarette, and saw no one was following me. It began to drift in on me that there really wasn't any reason why anyone should. I felt like kicking myself for letting Elizabeth plan the thing.

She'd insisted on my wearing gloves, which, I could see now, was a hell of a phony touch. She'd had me print out the ad in advance on a piece of dime-store paper, and that looked funny, too, when you put it with the other.

And then she'd figured out the exact price of the ad—only it wasn't the exact price.

I went on down the street toward film row, wondering why, since she always fouled me up, I ever bothered to listen to Elizabeth. Wondering whether I was actually as big a chump as she always said I was.

I wish now that I'd kept on wondering instead of plowing on ahead. But I didn't, and I don't think it proves I wasn't smart because I didn't.

2

When Elizabeth and I were married there was another show in Stoneville. It wasn't much of a house—five hundred chairs, and a couple of Powers projectors that should have been in a museum, and a wildcat sound system.

But it was a show and it pulled a lot of business from us, particularly on Friday and Saturday, the horse-opera nights. Not only that, it almost doubled the price of the product we bought.

In a town of seventy-five hundred people, you hadn't ought to pay more than thirty or thirty-five bucks for the best feature out. And you don't have to if you've got the only house. Where there's more than one, well, brother, there's a situation the boys on film row love.

If you don't want to buy from them, they'll just take their product across the street. And the guy across the street will snap it up in the hopes of freezing you out and buying at his own price the next year.

The fellow that owned the other house was named Bower. He's not around any more; don't know what ever did become of him. About the time his lease came up for renewal, I went to his landlord and offered to take over, paying all operating-expenses and giving him fifty per cent of the net.

Of course he took me up. Bower couldn't afford to make a proposition like that. Neither could I.

I gave Bower a hundred and fifty dollars for his equipment, which was a good price even if he didn't think so. Motion picture equipment is worth just about as much as the spot you have it in. It's tricky stuff to move; it's made to be put in a place and left there.

Well, Bower had about the same amount of stinker product under contract that I had. Part of it he'd bought because he couldn't help himself—we had block-booking in those days—and part because it would squeeze me.

Ordinarily, if he played it at all, he'd have balanced it up with good strong shorts. But there was a lot of it he couldn't have played on a triple bill with two strong supporting features.

What I did was to take his stinkers and mine and shoot 'em into the house, one after another. And I picked out shorts that were companion pieces, if you know what I mean. Inside of two months the house wasn't grossing five dollars a day.

The landlord was—he still is, for that matter—old Andy Taylor. Andy got his start writing insurance around our neck of the woods almost fifty years ago, and now he owns about half the county in fee and has the rest under mortgage. You could hear him crying in the next county when he saw what he was up against. But there wasn't a thing he could do.

He had the choice of taking twenty-five a month or fifty per cent of nothing, so you know what he took. I left the house standing dark, just like it is now.

No one but a sucker would think of trying to open a

third house under the circumstances, and he wouldn't have anything to play in it if he did. I buy all the major studio product and everything that's playable from the indies. Our house is on seven changes a week, and we actually change four or five times. The rest of the stuff we pay for and send back.

Our film bill only runs about thirty per cent more on the week than it used to, and our gross is about ninety per cent more. Of course, we've got to pay rent on the other house, and the extra express and insurance charges plus paper—advertising matter—runs into dough. But we've done all right. Plenty all right. We've got the most modern, most completely equipped small-city house in the state, and there's just one guy responsible.

Me.

I only book a month at a time. But booking with me for a month is equal to booking with the average exhibitor for three months; and the boys on the row don't exactly throw rocks at me.

I like to never have got away from the Playgrand exchange.

The minute I stepped in the door they rushed me back to the manager's office, and he just pushed his work aside and reached for the drinks.

They had some shorts in that he wanted my opinion on, so after a while we went back into the screening-room, which is just like a little theater, and checked them over. They were good stuff, some of the brightest, snappiest shorts I'd seen in a long time. Even with all I had on my mind I enjoyed them.

I've known the manager of Utopian since the days when he was on the road, and it was pretty hard to get away from there, too. And we got to talking baseball over at Colfax; and at Wolf I had to sit in on another screening and have another couple drinks.

I almost didn't book anything at Superior.

They had a complete new setup from booker to manager, and none of them knew straight up. They didn't even know who *I* was. I gave the booker three feature dates and five shorts, and I explained about six times that that was all I had open for the month. But he wouldn't give up. He reached over and took my date book right out of my hands.

"Why, here," he said. "We've made a mistake, haven't we? We've got an open date next Sunday."

"I've got something planned for that," I said.

"Now, let's see," he said. "What can we give you there? What do you say to—"

"That date's taken," I said.

"We'll fix that, get the other pic set out for you. You don't want an inferior picture in a Sunday spot when we can give you—"

Well, I don't mind seeing a man try to do his job, and all the row guys are pretty fast talkers. I'm a shade fast myself. I've never poked my tongue in my eyes, yet, though, and it's not because I close them when I talk.

I was about to tell him off in a nice way when the manager came out. He came up behind me and kind of worked his hand over my back like he was giving me a massage.

"Getting along all right?" he said. "Everything going to suit you, Mr. Barclay?"

I could feel myself turning red. "My name's not Barclay," I said.

"Oh," he said, stepping back a little, "I thought you were from Barclay Operating Company at—"

"I'm Joe Wilmot," I said. "I've operated Barclay for

the past ten years. The property's in my wife's name. Okay?"

He let out with a silly laugh, trying to pass it over, and made a grab for my hand.

"Mighty glad you came in, Joe. Anything we can do here for you, just say the word."

"You can't do a goddam thing for me," I said. "I won't pull out the dates I've given you because I'm in a hurry. But it'll be a hell of a long time before I give you any more."

"Now, Joe. Let's go back in the office and—"

"Go to hell," I said.

He and the booker both followed me to the door. I slammed it in their faces.

Every film row I've been around, there's at least one place like Chance Independent Releases, and one guy like Happy Chance. Not exactly, but you know what I mean.

They get ahold of maybe three or four features a year that you can throw in a middle-of-the-week spot, and a sex picture or two, and a few serials, and some stag-party shorts. They own the prints on the sex and stag stuff, and handle the other on commission for studios that don't have their own exchanges. Hap seemed to get by better than some of them, but Hap would. I've known him for more than twelve years, since he was working the booth in a grind-house, and I was driving film truck. And if he ever missed skinning anyone, I don't know when it was. He'd even skinned the Panzpalace chain; and when you skin a guy like Sol Panzer, who's run a ninety-three-house string up from a nickelodeon, you've got to be good.

I don't know why I liked Hap. Maybe it was the attraction of opposites, as they say in books.

"Glad you dropped in, laddie," he said, after we'd

sat down and the drinks were poured. "Been thinking about popping out to see you. How are things with the Barclay?"

"What's the use of kicking?" I said. "You wouldn't believe me."

"No, seriously. You must be coining it. How many changes are you on, anyway?"

I grinned at him over my glass. "All I need, Hap."

"Some chap was telling me the other day you were on more changes than any house in the state."

"I could be; I've got the product. I don't often make more than four a week though."

"Playing shutout with the rest?"

"That wouldn't be legal," I said. "They call that acting in restraint of trade."

"Uh-hah," he drawled. "Certainly. I should know you wouldn't be involved in anything like that."

"The town's wide open to anyone that wants to come in," I said. "I'll run all the good pix in the Barclay and all the stinkers in the Bower, and split the rest with the competition."

"Uh-*Hah!*" Hap let out a chuckle. "What's your house worth there, laddie, if you don't mind my asking?"

"Well, let's see. Ten times the annual return— between seventy-five and a hundred grand."

"It wouldn't possibly be worth a million, would it?"

"Not without a Sunday-night audience. We've got some good-looking gals out there."

"Just so, just so," he said.

"What's on your mind? Got a buyer for me?"

"We-ell—" He hesitated, frowning, plucking at the sleeve of his tweed suit. Hap goes for the English stuff right on down the line. And it doesn't suit him so bad—or so good. He sat there all diked out and talking

11

like a duke; and he turned his head a little and spit, and rubbed it into the carpet with one of his saddle-soaped shoes.

I wanted to laugh, but I knew I hadn't better. Hap isn't a good guy to have sore at you.

"Well, how about it?" I said.

"I guess not, laddie." He sighed and shook his head. "The proposition isn't quite big enough."

He looked at me a minute or two longer, and I thought he was going to say something more. But he didn't, and I didn't prod him. It wouldn't have done any good, and I thought I could see his angle, anyway.

"By the way," I said, "what'd you ever do with that sixteen-reeler? What do you call it—'Jeopardy of the Jungle'?"

Hap shrugged. "Oh, that goddam thing! Why, it hasn't been out of the can in months, laddie. It—" He broke off and gave me a sharp look. "Oh, you mean 'Jeopardy of the Jungle'!" he said. "It's going like wildfire. It's booked practically solid for the next three months."

I did laugh then. This was business, and I could.

"There aren't that many penitentiaries in the country," I said.

"Word of honor, Joe. The way it's been pulling 'em in even surprises me. You know I didn't care for it myself, even if it did have Gable and Bergman—"

"Yeah. A ten-frame shot of them sitting in the Stork Club. And what it has to do with the picture nobody knows."

"—but you can't argue with the b.o., Joe. The box office doesn't lie. Did you see last month's grosses in the *Herald?* The Empire grossed seven grand on 'Jep' the first—"

"I saw it," I said. "The only other attraction was Tommy Dorsey's orchestra."

"Let me show you something, Joe! Let me get out the *Herald*. I can show you small-city grosses for two days during the fall—"

"What two? Thanksgiving and Labor Day?"

"Okay," he said, "so it stinks."

"You know it does."

"But you want it."

"Well—" I said. And then I swallowed, and it was just like I'd forgotten how to talk.

A puzzled grin spread over Happy's face.

"Yeah," he said, "you want it. But why? You've already got more stuff than you can use. Tell Hap why you want it, laddie."

"Hell," I said, "use your head, Hap. This is the end of the season. We always get down toward the bottom of the pot at this time of year."

"Uh-hah. Mmm."

"Ordinarily I do have more product than I can play, but I've already let it go back. I don't have to have 'Jep.' I just thought I saw a nice spot for it next Sunday."

"'Jep' on *Sunday?*"

"Okay," I said, "I'm dumb. I was holding the spot for Superior, but they got me sore and I walked out."

He looked disappointed but not as much as I'd like to have seen him. There were still traces of that puzzled grin.

We settled on a price, and I got up to leave; and I stepped into it again right up to my neck.

"Aren't you forgetting something, old man?"

"You mean you want your rental now?" I said. "I don't play that way; I pay on delivery. You know that, Hap."

He shook his head.

"Well, what do you mean?"

"Paper," he said, as though he were talking to someone else. "First he books a stinker for Sunday, and then he starts to leave without so much as a one-sheet. Why would Joe Wilmot forget to buy paper?"

"I'll be damned," I said. "I guess that Superior crowd did get me upset."

"Uh-hah," he said. "Mmm."

I was so rattled that I let him sell me twice as much paper as I usually use. A dozen three-sheets, eighteen ones, and two twenty-fours. That and fifty window cards and the stuff for my lobby display.

I was shivering as I walked back to the hotel. Even thinking about Carol couldn't warm me up.

3

It was a Saturday morning, a little over a year ago, when I first saw Carol. We had a kids' matinee coming up at eleven o'clock and I was in the projection booth screening some stuff. I'd just made a change-over, and was putting a roll of film on the rewind.

Elizabeth waited for me to look around, but she finally saw I wasn't going to.

"This is Carol Farmer, Joe," she said. "She's going to stay with us."

"That's fine," I said, keeping my eye on the film.

"Our ladies' aid group is helping Carol attend business college," Elizabeth went on, "and she needed some place to cut down on expenses. I think we can use her very handily around the house, don't you?"

I still didn't look around. "Why not?"

"Thank you, dear," said Elizabeth, opening the door. "Come along, Carol. Mr. Wilmot has given you his approval."

I knew that she was laughing. She'd only brought Carol there to show me up. She didn't need my approval for anything.

Well, though, I passed old Doc Barrow, who runs the business college, on the street that afternoon; and he thanked me for being so generous in taking Carol in. I began to feel a little better, and kind of ashamed of the way I'd acted. Not on Elizabeth's account but Carol's.

She was about twenty-five and she'd spent most of her life on a two-by-four farm down in the sand flats, raising a bunch of brothers and sisters that ran off as soon as they got big enough to be any help. Her father was serving a five-year stretch for stealing hogs. Her mother was dead. Now, she was starting out to try to make something of herself.

We were changing programs the next day, and it was after midnight when I got home. But Carol was still up. She was sitting out at the kitchen table with a lot of books spread in front of her, and you could tell they didn't mean a thing to her. Not as much even as they would have to me.

She jumped up, all scared and trembling, like I'd caught her stealing. Her face got red, then white, and she snatched up a dish towel and began scrubbing at the table.

"Take it easy, kid," I said. "You're not on twenty-four-hour duty around here."

She didn't say anything; I don't guess she could. She stood watching me a minute, then she snatched up her books and sort of scuttled over to a corner and sat down on a stool.

She pretended to be studying, but I knew she wasn't. I knew it because I knew how she felt—because I'd felt the same way. I knew what it meant to be nothing and to want to be something. And to be scared out of your pants that someone is going to knock you down—not because of what you've done but because you can't strike back. Because they want to see you squirm, or they have a headache, or they don't like the way your hair is parted.

I opened the refrigerator door and took a look inside. It was full, as usual, with the leftover junk that passes for food with Elizabeth. Little plates of salad, bowls of consommé, sauce dishes of fruit, and nonfattening desserts. But way back in the rear I spotted a baked ham and a chocolate cake.

I took them over to the table, along with some bread and butter and a bottle of milk.

"You ain't—you're not supposed to eat that, Mr. Wilmot."

"Huh?" I almost dropped the carving-knife.

"Huh-uh. I mean, no, sir. Mrs. Wilmot said that was for tomorrow."

"Well," I said, "ain't that just dandy?"

"Yes, sir. There's some soup on the stove. That's what I-we—what we're supposed to have tonight."

I didn't argue about it. I just went over to the cupboard and got two plates, and I filled one of them so full it needed sideboards.

"Now, come over here," I said, "and eat this. Eat every damned bit of it. If there's any holler I'll say I did it."

Christ, I wish you could have seen her! She must have been empty all the way down. She didn't hog the food. She just sat and ate steadily, like she was going at a big job that needed doing. And she didn't mind my watching her. She seemed to know that I'd been the same way myself.

When she'd finished I told her to take her books and go to bed; and she said, "Yes, sir," and took off.

It made me a little uncomfortable for anyone to be so obedient, and yet I can't say I didn't like it, either. And it wasn't because I ever thought about telling her to do anything, well, anything bad. I just couldn't see the gal that way. I couldn't see her at all, if you know what I mean. If there was ever a woman that you wouldn't look at twice she was it. Probably she still is.

Because the more I think about it, the more I'm convinced that I'm seeing something that no one else can. And it took me three months before I could see it.

It was a Sunday afternoon. Elizabeth had taken her car and gone visiting, and I was lying down. We don't operate the house on Sunday afternoon. Local sentiment's against it.

There was a knock on my door, and I said, "Come in, Carol," and she came in.

"I just wanted to show you the new suit Mrs. Wilmot gave me," she said.

I sat up. "It looks very nice, Carol."

I don't know which I wanted to do most, laugh or cry.

She was a little bit cockeyed—maybe I didn't tell you? Well. And she was more than a little pigeon-toed. The suit wasn't new. It was a worn-out rag Elizabeth had given her to make over, and she'd botched it from top to bottom. And she had on a pair of Elizabeth's old shoes that didn't fit her half as well as mine would.

The blouse was too tight for her breasts, or her breasts were too big for the blouse, however you want to put it. They were too big for anything but an outsize. A good deep breath and she'd have had to start dodging.

I felt the tears coming into my eyes, and yet I wanted to laugh, too. She looked like hell. She looked like a sack of bran that couldn't decide which way it was going to fall.

And then the curtain rose or however you want to put it, and everything was changed.

And what I began to think about wasn't laughing or crying.

That tiny bit of cockeyedness gave her a cute, mad look, and the way she toed in sort of spread her buttocks and made a little valley under her skirt, and—and it don't—doesn't—make sense but there was something about it that made me think of the Twenty-Third Psalm.

I'd thought she looked awkward and top-heavy, and, hell, I could see now that she didn't at all. Her breasts weren't too big. Jesus, her breasts!

She looked cute-mad and funny-sweet. She looked like she'd started somewhere and been mussed up along the way.

She was a honey. She was sugar and pie. She was a bitch.

I said, "Come here, Carol," and she came there.

And then I was kissing her like I'd been waiting all my life to do just that, and she was the same way with me.

I don't know how long it was before I looked up and saw Elizabeth in the doorway.

4

I always stop at the Crystal Arms when I'm in the city. They know I pay for what I get, and no questions, and whenever they can do me a favor they don't hold back.

There wasn't anything in my room box but a few complimentary theater tickets. I gave them to the bell captain and took the elevator upstairs. The heat was just being turned on full, and the room was a little chilly. I dragged a chair up to the radiator and sat down with my coat and hat on.

I wasn't worried. Not too much. I guess I just had a touch of the blues. I had everything in the world to look forward to, and I had the blues. I got out part of a pint I had in my Gladstone, and sat down again.

The lights were coming on, blobbing through the misty night haze that hung over the city. Over in the yards a freight gave out with a highball. I took a drink and closed my eyes. I tried to imagine it was fifteen years ago, and I was on the freight, and I was looking at the city for the first time. And I thought, *Hell, if you had to be blue why not then instead of now?*

When I saw it was getting really dark I pulled myself together and changed my socks and shirt. I took the stairs down a couple of floors, and knocked on

Carol's door. The ventilator was open, and I could hear her splashing around in the tub.

"House dick," I said. "Open up."

She came to the door holding a big bath towel in front of her. When she saw it was really me—I—she dropped the towel and stood back for me to come in. She locked the door and walked over to the bed and lay down.

"That's all right," I said, sitting down by her. "You can put something on if you want to."

"Do you want me to?"

"I don't want you to catch cold," I said.

She said she wouldn't.

I gave her a drink out of the part of a pint, and lighted a cigarette for both of us. She sat up on one elbow and coughed and choked until I had to slap her on the back. I remembered then that I'd never seen her smoke before and that that was the first drink I'd ever given her.

"Is that the first time you smoked a cigarette?" I asked.

"Yes, Joe."

"And that's your first drink of liquor? What'd you take it for?"

"You gave it to me."

"Hell," I said, "you didn't have to take it."

There was a little finger of hair hanging down the middle of her forehead. She looked at it, turning her eyes in to be more cockeyed, and blew upward over her nose. The wisp of hair rose and settled down on her forehead again. I laughed and patted her on the bottom. I put my head down against her breast and squeezed. She freed one of her hands ...

We had supper in her room—club sandwiches, waffle potatoes, apple pie with cheese, and coffee. I stood in the closet when the waiter delivered it. She'd never seen waffle potatoes before. She kept turning them around in her fingers, and nibbling the squares off a little at a time.

"Did everything go all right today?" she said finally.

"Pretty good."

"Why are you worried, then? Did something happen at the newspaper office?"

"Nothing much," I said; and I told her about it. "It's a good joke on Elizabeth. She's always acted like we didn't have good sense, and—"

"Maybe we don't have."

"Huh?" I said. "What do you mean, Carol?"

She'd never spoken up much before, and it surprised me; and I guess I sounded pretty abrupt. She dropped her eyes.

"I'm afraid, Joe. I'm afraid Elizabeth's trying to get us into trouble."

"Why, that's crazy!" I said. "We're all in this together. She couldn't make trouble for us without making it for herself."

"Yes, she—I mean, I think she could," said Carol. "You and me have to do everything. We run all the risks."

"Well, but look," I said. "I admit I got pretty much up in the air at the time. But what's actually the worst that could have happened there at the newspaper office? All they could have done was to refuse to take the ad, isn't that right?"

She shook her head as though she hadn't heard me. "Anyway, she's trying to get me in trouble. Why did she have to have me register here as Mrs. J.J. Williamson?"

"Why not? We had to agree on some name so we

could reach you in case of emergency. You had to have some name to receive answers to the ad."

"But not *that* one, Joe. I got to thinking about it today; it's the same initials as yours. It kind of sounds like yours."

"Well—well," I said. I laughed, not very hard. "It's just a coincidence. What harm could it do, anyhow?"

She didn't answer me. She just shook her head again.

"If anyone made any boners it was me," I said, and I started telling her about Hap Chance. "It looked suspicious, see? With all the product I've got, why should I want sixteen reels of junk from him?"

Carol shrugged. "You explained it to him."

"Yeah, but it didn't look so good, particularly with me forgetting to buy paper."

"Well."

"It made it look like I didn't intend to play the picture. I almost might as well have told him I wanted that sixteen-reeler because of its length. Because it would make twice as hot a fire as—"

It wasn't true. The slip couldn't have meant anything like that to Hap, and Carol knew it. She saw I was just trying to divert her from Elizabeth.

We'd turned off all the lights except the one in the bathroom, and I was holding her on my lap in a big chair in front of the window. She began to breathe very deeply. I turned her face away from my chest, and I saw that she was crying.

"Don't do that," I said. "Please, Carol."

"Y-You're in love with her," she said. "She treats you like a dog, an'—and you go right on loving her."

"The hell I do!"

"Y-You do. And it's not fair! I'd do anything in the world for you, anything, Joe! And she hates you.

And—a-and it doesn't make any difference. Y-You k-keep right on—"

"But, damnit, I don't!"

"You do, too!"

It would have gone on all night, but I didn't let it.

As the guy said on his wedding night, it was no time for talking.

5

It was the next afternoon, and I was feeling pretty low.

Coming out of the city I'd passed a guy walking, a tired shabby-looking guy that looked like he needed a good night's sleep and a square meal; and I started to stop for him. And then, just when he was about to catch up with me, I stepped on the gas and drove off.

It was a mean thing to do and I hadn't intended doing it. What I meant to do was carry him down the road as far as he was going, and give him some food and change. Instead of that, I'd torn off when he almost had his hand on the door.

All of a sudden it came over me why I'd had so many blue spells lately. It was because I felt like I didn't amount to much any more. It was because I didn't feel that I was as good as other people—that I shouldn't put myself with people who wouldn't do what I was doing.

Subconsciously, I'd been afraid that hitchhiker might sense something, like maybe he'd pass up the car or ask to be let out after he got in. Subconsciously, I'd felt like he ought to.

I wondered again, like I had a thousand times, how the hell it all started.

One time, years ago, I sat in on one of Elizabeth's literary club meetings when they were discussing some lady poet. This poetry, this stuff this lady wrote, wasn't like real poetry. It wasn't like anything, in fact. It was just a lot of words strung together about God knows what all, and they'd say the same things over and over.

Well, though, it seemed like the stuff did make sense, once you understood what this lady was trying to do. She was writing about everything all at one time. She was writing about one thing, of course, more than the others, but she was throwing in everything that was connected with it; and she didn't pretend to know what was most important. She just laid it out for you and you took your choice.

I'll have to do the same thing.

Offhand, you'd say it began with Elizabeth catching Carol and me together that Sunday afternoon. But if there was a murder every time a husband or wife got caught like that there wouldn't be any people left. So—

It might have begun with the time I closed up Bower's house, and moved part of his equipment up to our garage. Or the time, right after we were married, when Elizabeth and I each took out twelve thousand five hundred dollars' insurance on the other. Or the time when I was delivering film for the exchanges, and it was raining, and I drove her up to her house in the company truck.

It may have started with Carol's old man being pinched for stealing hogs. Or the pushing around I took in reform school. Or at the orphanage—although it wasn't so bad there. The head matron was an old Irishwoman, weighing about three hundred pounds and so cross-eyed she scared me stiff the first time I saw her. But an angel couldn't have been any better.

But— Well, I'll tell things the best way I can.

One night I lost my key ring and couldn't lock up the show. Elizabeth wasn't in the house and she carried her keys with her, so I went out to the garage, upstairs, where she was checking some film.

"You don't need to do that," I said. "I can look that over in the morning before we open up."

"I'm quite capable of doing it."

"I didn't say you weren't."

"Thank you," she said. "I'm glad you feel I'm still of some value."

"Okay, be stubborn," I said. I took the keys and started to leave. "Where's the new cord for that motor?"

She looked blank.

I told her I'd bought a new cord and laid it by her breakfast plate that morning. "I thought you'd have sense enough to know what it was for. That cord's got a short in it."

"Why, how gallant of you, Joe!" she said. But she was scared.

I got the new cord and changed it, and threw the old one in the trash bucket. But the next time I was out there I saw that she'd dug it out and put it on one of the metal shelves.

And now that I think of it, it might have begun with her mother. The old lady never threw anything away. For months after she died, Elizabeth and I were throwing out balls of string and packages of wrapping-paper and other junk.

I don't know. It's hard to know what to put down and what to leave out.

There was a lot of stuff on the radio and in the newsreels and newspapers. People getting run over, blown up, drowned, smothered, starved, lynched. Mercy killings, hangings, electrocutions, suicides. People who didn't want to live. People who deserved killing. People who were better off dead.

I don't suppose it was any different from usual, any different from what it always has been and always will be. But coming then, right at that time, it kind of tied in.

Day after day and night after night, there was a row. With one breath Elizabeth would tell us to get out; with the next she was threatening what she'd do if we tried.

"What the hell do you want?" I'd yell. "Do you want a divorce?"

"Be publicly displaced by a frump like that? I think not."

"Then I'll clear out. Carol and I."

"What with? And how would I run the show?"

"We'll sell the show."

"We can't. We couldn't get a fraction of its value from an outsider. I'm willing to give you credit, Joe. You're at least half the business."

That was true. A showman would know that. Anyone that was a showman wouldn't want to buy.

"I think I get you," I said. "You want me to give up any claim I've got on the business. Then you could peddle out at any old price and still have a nice wad."

She raised her eyebrows. "Such language, Joe! What would your parents think?"

"Goddam you!"

"How much, Joe? What will you give me to leave you in undisputed possession of the field?"

"You know damned well I haven't any money."

"So you haven't. Mmm."

There was more talk. Carol and me talking by

ourselves. Elizabeth and me talking. The three of us talking together. Nagging and lashing out, and getting madder and edgier. And the stuff in the newspapers, and the newsreels, and on the radio. There were some Canadian travel folders, and a farmer's wife over in the next county who stumbled into a tubful of hot lard and was burned unrecognizably. There were the premiums on those insurance policies falling due. Twelve thousand five hundred dollars—double indemnity.

Then there was Elizabeth saying, "Well, Joe. I've finally hit upon a nice round sum."

And me, kind of shaking inside because I knew what the sum was, and trying to sound like I was kidding. "Yeah, I suppose you want about twenty-five thousand bucks."

There must have been something else, but I can't think of it now.

6

Our house, the show, I mean, is just four doors off of Main Street. On the corner, on our side and fronting on Main, is a dime store. On the opposite corner, cater-cornered from us, is the Farmers' Bank. Down the street a block is the City Hotel, and next door to it is the bus station and a garage.

I'm not taking credit for picking the location, but I couldn't have picked a better one if I'd done it. Any time you can get close to a bank, a hotel, a garage, a bus station, and a dime store—above all, a dime store—you've got something.

The average person might think a Main Street location would be better, but it wouldn't. It's too hard to park on Main.

I sat in the car a minute after I parked, feeling kind of good and proud like I always do when I look at the house. It's not as big as some city houses, but there's nothing to come up to it in a town of our size. And it's my baby. I built it all out of nothing.

We've got a copper-and-glass marquee that you couldn't duplicate for five grand, although naturally I didn't pay that. I had the job done by an out-of-town firm, and it just so happened that they couldn't get the work okayed by our local building inspectors. You know what I mean. So I settled for five hundred, and that, plus a few bucks for the inspectors, was all the marquee cost me.

The lobby is fifteen feet deep, spreading out fan shape from the double doors, with a marble-and-glass box office in the center. There's a one-sheet board on each side of the box office, glassed in with gold frame. The lobby walls have a four-foot marble base. The upper half is glass panels for display matter, with mirrors spotted in every three feet.

There's a carpet running from each door to the street.

That carpet would cost fifteen dollars a yard, but I got it for nothing. I was the first showman in this territory to lay a carpet through his lobby. I sold the equipment house on the idea, showed them how it would be opening up a big new market, so they put it in for me. Of course, I let them take a picture of me in front of the house, and I gave them a testimonial and an estimate on the number of miles that had been walked on the carpet without it showing any wear.

The house doesn't have a balcony. The ceiling's too low. I don't mean we're cramped. We're twenty feet at the entrance, which is four feet higher than the average show ceiling. But it's not high enough for a balcony.

We've only got a ninety-five-foot shot from the projection booth to the screen, and the floor can't drop much more than an inch to the foot. I'd have to double the pitch for a balcony, and even now it hurts people's necks to sit in the front row.

We get along pretty well without a balcony, anyway. I've got four rows of seats on tiers at the back of the house, extending up to the projection booth. Not full rows, of course, on account of the entrance and exit and the aisle down the middle from the booth door. It's more like loges.

When I put them in my customer liability insurance jumped a hundred dollars a year, because you can't tell when some boob might fall and break his neck. But the extra seating-space is worth it.

Jimmie Nedry, my projectionist, was just making a change-over when I went into the booth. He started the idle projector and put a hand on the sound control. At just the right instant he jerked the string that opens one port and closes the other. He pulled the switch on the first projector, lifted out the reel of film, and put it on the rewind. There wasn't a break of even a fraction of an instant. You'd have thought the picture all came in one reel.

"Well, Jimmie," I said, "how's it going?"

He didn't say anything for a minute, but I knew he was nerving himself up to it. I feel sorry for Jimmie. Any way I can I try to help him out. I've got his oldest girl ushering for me, and I use his boys as much as possible in putting out paper.

"Look, Mr. Wilmot," he blurted out suddenly. "Grace and me were talking last night, and we was wondering if you couldn't put her on selling tickets. She could sit down that way, and people wouldn't see that she was—couldn't see much of her. And—"

"I'd like to have Grace," I said. "But you know how I'm tied up. I just about have to use women from the Legion auxiliary. If it wasn't for that I'd jump at the chance to take Grace."

"We got to have a little more money, Mr. Wilmot. If you could use the boys some on the door, or taking care of the—"

"I've got to spread that work around for the high

school team. I'm doing all I can for you, Jimmie," I said.

"Well," he said. And he hesitated again. "I got to have some more money."

"There's no way I can give it to you," I pointed out. "You're classified as a relief operator. The union only allows me to work you twenty-four hours a week."

"You mean that's what you pay me for," he snapped. "I'm actually workin' about sixty!"

"That's all I can pay you for," I said. And it was true. The unions really keep an eye on social security records. "If you don't want the job perhaps you'd better quit."

"Yeah?" he grunted. "Where the hell would I get another one?"

"As a projectionist?"

"That's my line. It's the only thing I've ever done."

"Well, that makes it tough," I said. "If you had a couple grand for transfer and initiation fees, you might get into another local. But the chances are all against it."

He gave me a sore look, started to say something, then turned back to the machines. I went back downstairs and outside.

I was standing out near the curb, just lighting a cigarette, when a big black roadster pulled up and Mike Blair got out. He was the last man in the world I wanted to see. He's a business agent for the projectionists' union, and I'd seen more than enough of him six years before when this town was in his territory.

We shook hands, neither of us putting much pressure into it, and I asked him where he was headed. He pushed his hat back on his head, taking his time about answering and giving me a mean grin.

He took the cigar out of his mouth, looked at it, and put it back in again.

"I'm already there, Joe. This town's back in my district."

"Yeah?" I said. "I mean—it is?"

"Nice, huh?" He waggled the cigar in the corner of his mouth. "In fact, it's been back in my district for three days. I was over here last night, looking the old burg over, and the night before."

"Well," I said, "it's funny I didn't see you."

"It'd been a hell of a lot funnier if you had. Don't kid me, Joe. I like you in a nasty sort of way, but I don't like to be kidded. You were out of town."

"I couldn't help it. I—"

"I don't give a damn about that. You remember what I told you at the time I left here? What I told you a dozen other times?"

"Well—"

"I'll tell you again for the last time. You're an indie. You can run your own projectors and use a card man for reliefs, and we'll carry you on the fair list. You do that or else. You do it or put two men in the booth. Full time."

"Now, look, Blair," I said, "let's be reasonable about this. You—"

"We ain't got time to reason, Joe. Jimmie Nedry's already run over his twenty-four hours."

"But how can I run the projectors and the house, too? Just show me how, Blair, and I'll—"

"Maybe you can't. I'll send you down another operator, and you keep out of the booth. How's that?"

He knew how it was without asking. Two full-time operators would cost me a hundred and eighty bucks a week.

"Look," I said. "Where did you get that two men to

the booth and ninety-dollar scale to begin with? I'll tell you. Panzpalace framed it for you to freeze out city competition. They could carry four men at a hundred and fifty if they had to, but the indies couldn't, so you guys threw in with them. I—"

"Look who's talking," he said. "Well?"

"I can't pay it," I said. "Goddamit, you know I can't."

"Get up in the booth, then, and stay there. All but twenty-four hours of the week."

"I can't do that, either."

He grinned, nodded, and walked off. I had to follow him out to his car.

"You're going to pull the house?"

"You know I am, Joe."

"After all I've done for union labor in this town, you're going to—going to—" I couldn't go on. The look on his face stopped me.

"Why, you chiseling son of a bitch," he said softly. "You got the nerve to talk about what you've done for union labor. You get them to practically put you up a new house for nothing, and—"

"I paid scale all the way through the job."

"Sure you did. With coupon books. And the coupons weren't even good for full admissions; just a ten-cent discount. The boys put in an eight-hour day for you, and got out and sold tickets at night. That's what it amounted to. They built you a new house and then kept it packed for you."

"They all got their money. I didn't hear any of them kicking about it."

"Okay, Joe," he said. "It's none of my business, anyway. But this other is. You're off the fair list starting tomorrow."

Maybe you don't know what it means to have a

house struck in a town like ours. It means you settle fast or go broke. There'd be spotters from every local watching out front. Any time a union man or a member of his family bought a ticket, it would mean a twenty-five buck fine for him. Consequently, in a place where everyone knows everyone else, there wouldn't be any bought.

"All right," I said. "But I'd like to ask you a couple of questions, Blair."

"As many as you like, Joe."

"When did your men take out cards in the bricklayers' union?"

"Huh?" He blinked. "What do you mean?"

"I'm talking about the job your boys did in the house over at Fairfield last week."

"Oh, that!" He forced a laugh. "Why that wasn't a bricklayer's job. All it amounted to was putting a few bricks under the projectors. Leveling them up. They had to make a longer shot, see, and—"

"It was brick work, wasn't it?"

"But the bricklayers couldn't have done it. The operators had to!"

"Then you should have had bystanders in from the bricklayers," I said. "You know what I think, Blair? I think the bricklayers are going to file a complaint against you with the state federation. I think that brick work at Fairfield is going to have to be torn out and done over by the proper local."

He stopped grinning, and his face fell a little. "You get around, don't you, Joe?"

"More than you'd think," I said. "More than you do, apparently. Did you know that the projectionists at View Point installed over fifty seats in the house there?"

"Sure I know about it," he snapped. "There wasn't

enough carpenters to do the job so the projectionists finished it up."

"Why didn't the carpenters work overtime?"

"Because the chairs had to be in for the night show!"

"I get you," I said. "Rules are rules until they start pinching you. Then you throw them out the window."

He stood at the side of his car, thinking, bobbling the cigar around in his mouth. The bricklayers and carpenters are our two biggest locals; they're usually the biggest locals in any district. If they took a notion to—and Blair knew they would after I got through needling 'em—they could make him wish he'd never been born.

"Okay, Joe," he said, finally. "Maybe I was a little hasty."

"I thought you'd see it my way," I said. "No hard feelings?"

"All kinds of 'em." He looked down at my hand and shook his head. "I'm not through with you, Joe. Some day I'm going to hang one on you that you can't squirm out of."

7

Our house, our residence, sits out on the edge of town, almost a hundred yards from the highway. It's all that's left of the old Barclay homestead, just the house and a couple acres of ground and the outbuildings.

It was a little after midnight when I got there. I parked the car in the yard, in back of Elizabeth's, locked it up, and went in the kitchen door. The coffee percolator was going, and there was some cheese and pickles and other stuff sitting out on the table. I went through the door to the dining-room and started up the stairs.

"Oh, there you are, darling!" called Elizabeth.

She was sitting in the living-room with a book in her lap, and the light turned low.

"Wasn't it nice of me to wait up for you?" she said. "I've even fixed a lunch. I know you must be famished."

She had on a little gingham house dress, and she was smiling, and for a minute I was crazy enough to think she wasn't giving me a rib. Then I thought of all the times in the past she'd picked me up just to slap me down; and I went on upstairs without speaking.

I washed, combed my hair, and went back down again.

"All right," I said, "spit it out. What's up?"

"Don't you want something to eat, Joe?"

"I've ate—eaten," I said.

"Did you ate—eat—with Carol?"

"Pour it on me," I said. "I'm used to it. Hell, how could I eat with Carol? I left the city this morning."

"I hope you weren't foolish enough to register in together, Joe."

"No, we didn't. I don't know just when Carol registered. Just after the bus got there, I guess."

She sat staring at me, not speaking; her head thrown back, her eyes half closed. I told her about the bonehead she'd pulled on the price of the ad; and she only shook her head a little, as if nothing I could say would be of any importance.

After a long time she said, kind of talking to herself, "No, it's true. It *is* true."

"What's true?"

She held out her hand. "Let me see your date book, Joe."

I tossed it to her. It fell on the floor and she picked it up. She turned the pages to the month's bookings.

"I see Playgrand has been consulting you again," she said. "I hope you received a suitable fee?"

"Those are good shorts," I said. "After all, we've got to buy from someone, don't we?"

"Now, what did we do at Utopian?" she said. "Did we give him a third of our feature bookings because he's an old friend of ours? Or were we just a teeny-weeny bit—ah—intoxicated?"

"All right," I said. "I do give my friends the breaks. What's the difference as long as it don't lose us any money? You never saw me lose money helping a friend, did you?"

"No, Joe, I never did. And you never lost any in striking back at any enemy. But tell me. What did they say to you at Superior? Didn't they know you were the great Joe Wilmot—sole proprietor of his wife's property?"

"They didn't say anything. That was all the dates I had open."

"Really?"

"Yeah, rahlly," I said. "And I wouldn't push that wife's-property business too far. All you had when I met you was a run-down store building and a couple of hundred seats that weren't worth the chewing-gum that was stuck on them."

She shook her head, smiling that set, funny smile. "It's weird, isn't it? Positively fantastic."

"Goddamit," I said, "if there's something there you don't like, say so. We can change it easy enough."

"But I do like it, Joe! I like—I wasn't criticizing. I was only evaluating. Weighing things, I suppose you'd say."

"I don't know what you're talking about," I said. "And that's only half the story."

"Stupid," she said. "Yes, actually stupid. That with everything else. Vain, vindictive, lying, dishonest, a philanderer. And stupid. And yet—"

"You've left out a couple," I said. "Repulsive and nauseating."

She nodded. "Yes, Joe. I left them out."

She seemed to be waiting for me to say something, sitting there smiling at me, her hands caressing the arms of the chair.

"You're slipping," I said. "I'm going to eat something and go to bed."

"Joe!"

I turned in the doorway. She was standing. It looked like she had started to follow me.

"Well, what?" I said.

"Nothing, Joe. I guess—nothing."

I went on into the kitchen.

I fixed a sandwich and a cup of coffee. When I'd got away with about half of it the lights blinked, went dim, and came on full again.

It didn't register on me for a second. Then it was as if something was holding me back when I tried to move.

It seemed like I was about to see something; I mean I could almost see what it was. And it scared me so badly my stomach rolled and my scalp crawled. I came alive and stumbled to the door. I half fell down the back steps and ran for the garage. I raced up the outside stairs and threw myself against the door.

The room was lined with sheet metal. Floors, ceiling, walls. The projectors and sound tables I'd got from Bower were stashed in a corner. In the center of the room was the metal film table, with a reel at each end and a quarter-horse motor at one.

There was a metal stool in front of the table, and Elizabeth was seated on it, bent over. Her face wasn't six inches from the film that was traveling in front of her.

Two full reels were lying on the table next to the motor. They were partly unwound, and their ends dangled down into the open film can. There were seven more reels in it. It was a full-length feature, seven in the can, two on the table, and one in the rewind. A can with a two-reel travelogue and one with a one-reel cartoon were under the table. Close to Elizabeth's feet. They were standing open, too.

The film was wet. As it passed through the reel it sent a fine spray over the motor. The spray formed a trickle that ran down the pear-shaped back of the motor.

The cord sparked.

The trickle of water seemed to catch fire.

There was a flash as if someone had tossed a barrel of yellow paint into the room.

I struck out with my hand, and something seemed to grab it and push my arm back into my shoulder. A streak of lightning shot across the table. There were a couple of pinwheels of fire at each end. Then, a loud *pop* and darkness; and the sound of the broken film whipping against the table.

And Elizabeth crying.

I found the cord and jerked it loose. I fumbled along the wall until I found the circuit breaker, and the lights came on again.

I turned them off and opened the door. I picked up Elizabeth and carried her back to the house and into the kitchen. I put my foot up on a chair, and pulled her over my knee, and whaled the tar out of her.

She stopped crying and laughing, and really began to cry.

Some way she got turned around and put her arms around my neck.

8

You wouldn't think we'd have been hungry, but we were. We ate some sandwiches and coffee; and afterward she made me go upstairs to the bathroom with her to get my hand fixed up.

It wasn't a bad burn; it just looked bad. But she insisted on doping it all up, so I let her.

"What'd you want to do a crazy thing like that for?" I asked. I'd asked her about umpteen times already.

"You know why," she said.

"No, I don't, either."

"Well, you do," she said. Like a little girl. And she did look like one then. Her skin was always so clear you could almost see through it, and now it was rosy and flushed.

She acted like she was afraid to look at me; bashful, you know. She'd duck her head and look the other way. Her hair was like silk as she bent over my hand. Black silk, with a finger-wide streak of white through the center.

"You're awfully pretty," I said, all of a sudden.

"I'll bet I'm black and blue."

"Let's see if you are."

"Now, Joe—don't—"

But she didn't pull away.

I put a kiss on my hand and patted her.

"Feel better now?"

"Uh-huh. And now you're going to bed."

"We've got some talking to do first," I said.

"All right," she said. "But just a little. I know you're worn out."

I didn't know why she blushed; why she didn't want to talk. Not right then, I didn't. I should have, sure, but you know how it is. You don't think about water when you're not thirsty.

She sat on the edge of the bed while I undressed and lay down.

"Now, what's it all about?" I said.

"I don't know, Joe. It just seemed at the moment that it was the only thing to do."

"We don't have to go through with this business," I said. "Maybe we can think of something else."

"Do we have to think of something else, Joe?"

"What—how do you mean?"

She was leaning back on one elbow, her legs drawn up under her. She lifted her eyes and gave me a long, slow look. She didn't answer.

"Well—well, maybe we don't have to," I said. "Gosh, Elizabeth, I don't know—I don't know what to do or what not to do. I never have known."

"I know I'm terribly difficult," she said. "No, I mean it. But I do hope you understand my intentions were good."

"Oh, sure," I said. "I understand."

"I'm afraid you don't," she said and laughed, "but we'll not argue about it. It's no longer important now. I hope it will never become important again."

"Tell me something," I said. "About what we were going to do. Did you feel like I did—like you wouldn't want to have other people around you any more? Like you'd be ashamed, not for yourself but for them?"

"Well—"

"I guess I'm not sure of what I mean myself," I said. "It wasn't the idea of breaking the law or not going to heaven. I didn't really see how we were doing anything very wrong. If it was someone you knew it would be different. If it was someone that was, well, respectable and a valued citizen and all that, it would be different. But when it's not—Well, if you can sacrifice—If three people can have happiness and go ahead and amount to something just by someone—someone that doesn't stand a show of being anyone or doing anything— getting out of the way, why—"

"I'll tell you why you felt as you did," said Elizabeth. "It was too simple."

"No, that wasn't—" I hesitated. "I don't think I get you, Elizabeth."

"We're strong people, Joe. Stronger at least than many. Without being too flattering we can say that we have good minds, good bodies, a good financial position."

"Not good enough."

"There's room for improvement," said Elizabeth. "There usually is. And there comes a time when the improvement seems imperative. So what do we superior people do? How do we exercise our fine talents in the emergency? We don't. We don't use them at all. We do something that the first man could have done much better. Something that anyone could do. We—we push over someone who is more trusting or less strong than we are."

"Well," I said, "it was the only thing we could think of."

"Yes, Joe. It was the only thing we could think of."

I frowned, and I suppose she thought I was getting mad.

"You go to sleep now, dear," she said. "We'll talk more later."

She got up and pulled down the shades, and turned off the light. She came back and bent over me, her face flushed, looking more like a little girl than ever.

"Think you can sleep, Joe?" she said.

And before I could answer, she lay down by my side and pulled my head against her breast.

We lay there for a long time. Long enough to give me every chance in the world. And I could feel her growing stiffer and older by the minute.

She didn't get mad.

She just acted sorry and sort of resigned. She moved away from me, and stood up.

"When was it, Joe?"

"I don't know what you're talking about," I said.

"Was it before you came here—to me?"

"Hell," I said, "you knew how it was all along. You've known about it for months."

"I didn't *know* until now, Joe. But that isn't the point. I'd have sworn this would be one time when, as you'd put it, you'd pass up a bet. If it wasn't, well, then there'll never be such a time. You've got nothing to share with me. There's nothing I can do for you."

As she started for the door I said, "Well, what do you want to do? Do you still want to go through with it?"

"By all means," she said. "I've changed my mind about its being too simple for us."

I let her go. I'd gone a little goofy when I thought she was in danger. But I should have known we couldn't patch things up. I still wasn't hot for the killing—who would be?—but if that was the only way to lead a happy, decent life, why ...

9

If you're like I am you've probably spotted a thousand couples during your lifetime that made you wonder why and how the hell they ever got together. And if you're like I used to be you probably lay it to liquor or shotguns.

Not that I can tell you why I married Elizabeth or she married me. Not exactly. But I can tell you this. We both knew exactly what we were getting, barring a few points, and we went right ahead and made the grab anyway.

And looking back it all seems perfectly natural.

That first rainy night when I drove her home in the film truck she got out, fumbled in her purse, and handed me fifty cents.

"No, I want you to take that, Joe," she said, when I sort of began to stutter. "It would have cost me much more than that to take a cab."

"But—but look here, Miss Barclay—"

"Good night, Joe. Be careful of the flower beds when you drive out."

I told her what she could do with her flower beds and four-bit pieces. I told her she could walk in mud up to her ears before I gave her another ride. I—

But I was ten miles down the road when I did it. At

the time I couldn't think of any more to say than I can now when she ties me into knots. Not as much, maybe, because I hadn't had any practice.

My next run-in with her was a Sunday, about two weeks later. I was still sore, or thought I was; but when she motioned me over to the box office I went running, like a dog running for a bone.

"Come around to the door," she said, "you're in the way of the patrons there." And I went around. Then, she said, "I want you to do an errand for me, Joe." And I said, "Well—well, thank you."

"A whole row of seats has broken down," she went on. "I want you to go over to the Methodist Church and pick up thirty of their folding chairs. I've already called about them."

I gulped and got started so fast I didn't really understand what she'd told me. I heard it, you know, but I didn't understand it. And when I did, or thought I did, I still couldn't believe it.

I got the chairs after some pretty chilly looks from the parson, and took them back and set them up. By that time I was so late on the route that a couple of hours more wouldn't make any difference, so I found a little engine trouble, and I'd just got it fixed when the show closed for the night. So I drove her home again.

She didn't hand me fifty cents that night. She said something about not having any change—I knew she had a five-pound sack full—and that she'd pay me some other time.

"I'll settle cheap," I said, bracing myself. "Tell me—I mean, can I ask you a question?"

"Certainly you may."

"Were those chairs you got tonight—were they some you'd loaned to the church?"

"No. I thought I mentioned they were theirs."

"You mean," I said, "you borrowed thirty chairs from a church for a picture show on Sunday night?"

She frowned a little, then her face cleared. "You mean they might have been using them? Oh, but I knew they wouldn't be. That church never has anything approaching a crowd on Sunday night."

"Well," I said, "well, that makes everything just dandy."

I found out later that her old man, her grandfather rather, had donated the sites for most of the churches in town, so I guess she felt like they owed her a few favors and they apparently felt the same way.

Jesus, what a hell of a way to collect! It was like asking to sleep with a man's wife because he owed you five dollars.

After that, after I really began to notice things, to do something besides set the film cans in the lobby and beat it, I saw her head for one jam after another. And instead of pointing my nose the other way, I'd jump in and try to give her a straight steer.

She had trouble spelled all over her. She'd always have it. And I knew it, and I didn't want it any different—then.

You don't buy a twenty-three-jewel watch and hope to turn it into an alarm clock. I didn't have any idea of ever changing her.

The funniest deal came up one night over some color film.

She was using Simplex projectors with nine hundred-watt Mazdas, and the way the stuff came out on the screen was pretty God-awful. Most of the time you could tell the men from the women characters but they all looked like they'd been brawling in a jelly closet.

"I'm going to make them give me a rebate on this,"

she told me. "I've never seen such a thing in my life!"

"You won't get any rebate," I said. "This print is brand new; that's the trouble with it. What little color stuff you've played in the past has been old and those Mazdas would shoot through it. But there's more and more color coming in, and you'll probably be getting a lot of new prints."

"Oh?" she began to look a little sick. "What should I do, Joe?"

"Get rid of the lamps and put in carbon arcs. They'll cut through anything."

"Are they—pretty expensive?"

"Well, it's going to cost you something to convert, sure," I said. "But you should be able to squeeze around that. Talk it over with your power-and-light man here. Show him how the arcs will burn more juice and it's to his advantage for you to have them. If you handle it right you might be able to get him to put them in for you."

She brightened up and said she'd try it.

Two weeks later she was still using lamps, and from what little I could get out of her I knew she'd keep right on using them as far as the manager of the power-and-light company was concerned.

Well, I picked a light night on the route, drove to beat hell for sixteen hours straight, and got back into Stoneville early the next morning. I brushed up a little bit and paid a call on the power company.

Not that I'd expected him to be, but the manager wasn't an imbecile or a boor or a grafter. He was just a pretty pleasant citizen who'd spent a lot of time learning his business. And he wasn't going to let anyone tell him where to get off, even if he had been trotting around town with his tail sticking out at a time when she had six dresses for every day in the week.

I don't know what I said to him. Nothing in particular, I guess. We sat around and talked for thirty minutes or so and went out and had coffee together, and that was all there was to it. Two days later the arcs went in.

I could tell you some more things along the same line, but there wouldn't be too much point to it. The time's better used, probably, in mentioning that she'd found out plenty about me. About all there was to find out.

Her mother was pretty feeble, and I used to inquire about her. So sooner or later, of course, she had to inquire about mine—about my folks. And that brought up the orphanage, and one thing led to another. At first I told her I'd picked up the projectionist trade when I was in the orphanage. But then I remembered telling her I'd skipped out of the joint when I was fourteen, and, rather than look like a liar, I told her the truth.

"Was the reform—the industrial school very bad, Joe?"

"I thought it was at the time," I said. "But after I saw a few—"

I told her about the jails.

I told her how it was when you really got down to the bottom of the pot, how you'd get seventy-two hours on vagrancy as soon as you hit a town, how they'd float you back on the road again before you could get a job or even a good meal in your belly.

"I'm never going to go back to stuff like that," I said. "They'll have to kill me first."

"Or?" she said.

"Yeah," I said. "It'll be 'or' before they get me down again."

I didn't have to tell her why I was sticking to what

looked like a pretty cheap job, because I knew she knew. Maybe she didn't know any more about business and public relations than a two-year-old. But she could see an angle a mile off, particularly where it concerned me. Most of the time it was like we were looking out the same window.

There were around fifty customers on my route. They bought product on everything from a two-day to a week's option. I mean it was their right to keep it for a week if they wanted to, which didn't mean that they always would. They just bought a long option to play safe.

Well, suppose they decided to keep it four days or less, then turned it back to me for pick-up. I take it on down the road a ways and give another house a run on it for half price. The house is able to make one more change on the week than it's been making and I pick up a ten spot or so.

I had to be careful. Bicycling film *is* a penitentiary offense. But a guy that's actually hauling the product—a guy that knows just who is buying from where—can get away with it. The exchanges can't afford to check the small towns. They've maybe got a damned good idea they're being roped, but unless it gets too bad they let it go.

I never let it get too bad.

Well, there's not a lot more to tell.

Stoneville wasn't important enough as a show town then for the union to bother with, and Elizabeth had a punk boy working in the booth. One of those sharp lads who has to think ten or fifteen minutes before he can decide which end of the match to strike.

His best trick was to get the reel in backward or out of sequence, but he had a lot of others. Missing changeovers. Forgetting to turn the sound on. Hitting the arcs before the film was rolling.

It was the last one that finally got me.

By this time I'd rearranged my route so that Stoneville was my last stop instead of the first one; and I'd stay there overnight before going back to the city—Sure, at a hotel. Where do you think?

Anyway, I was sitting in the house that night when I finally got just as much of that punk as I could take. He'd already run one reel backward. He'd missed two change-overs, and he'd turned the sound on full and forgot about it. That's more boners than a good projectionist will pull in a lifetime, but the punk wasn't through yet. Right after the second miss, he caught the film on fire.

If you've gone to many picture shows, particularly back in the early days of the business, you've seen it happen once or twice. The film will hit the screen like a still. Then it looks like someone is punching a live cigar butt through it from the back.

That's caused by not having the film rolling while the arcs are on. Because those arcs are just like a blast furnace, and nothing burns as easily or faster than film.

Projectors are fixed so that nothing but the film in the frame can burn. But not everyone knows that, and even if they did—what the hell? No one's going to thank you for not roasting them. No one's going to pay dough to sit in a dark house while some boob splices film.

I climbed up into the booth without saying a word, and the punk didn't ask me anything. I just took the splicing-knife and the glue pot away from him, tied the film back together, and started the projector rolling again. Then I walked over to him and stood up close. He wasn't home talent. Any trouble that was made would have to come from him.

"Which way do you want to go out of here?" I said. "Walking or sliding?"

Before he could say what he was getting ready to—that I couldn't fire him and that if Elizabeth paid him better dough he'd do a better job—I slapped him. I gave him the old cop trick. A slap for taking up my time, a slap for not answering questions, a slap because he couldn't answer 'em, a slap because it hurt my hand, a slap because he was such a sickening-looking son of a bitch with the blood running out of him. And a dozen good hard ones on general principles.

I shoved fifteen bucks at him, his week's pay, told him to go out the exit and keep going, and tossed his coat and hat after him. That's the last I saw of him from that day to this.

When the box office closed and Elizabeth came up, I was still sore enough to tell her what I'd done. The details.

"Do you think that was necessary, Joe?" Her eyebrows went up.

"What the hell can he do?" I said. "He's too scared to sue, and he doesn't have any friends or family here."

"Joe," she said. "Ah, Joe."

I drove her home and sat in the kitchen while she made coffee and sandwiches. She'd hardly spoken a word since we'd left the show, and she didn't say much more until the food was ready. Then she sat down across from me, studying, her chin in her hand.

"How much money have you, Joe?" she said at last.

I told her I had a little over two grand, around twenty-one fifty.

"Well, I haven't any," she said. "No more than my

operating capital. On top of that I can't go on much longer without at least a little new equipment, and on top of that there's a fifteen-hundred-dollar past-due mortgage on this house."

"I'll lend you the money," I said. "You can have anything I've got. I'll get you a decent projectionist, too."

"For fifteen a week, Joe?" She shook her head. "And I couldn't take a loan from you. I'd never be able to pay it back."

"Well—" I hesitated.

"I'm a good ten years older than you are, Joe."

"So what?" I said. "Look—are we talking about the same thing? Well, then put it this way. I'll run your machines until we can train some local kid to do a halfway decent job. I'll get a couple weeks' vacation and do it. And you can have the money as a gift or you can take it as a loan. Hell, you can't ever tell when your luck will change. But as far as—"

"Joe, I don't—"

"—but I'm not buying any women," I said. "Not you, anyhow."

She looked at me and her eyes kept getting bigger and blacker, and there were tears in them and yet there was a smile, too, a smile that was like nothing I'd ever seen before or ever got again—from her or anyone else.

"You're good, Joe," she said. "I hope you'll always hold on to that thought. You are good."

"Aw, hell," I said. "You've got me mixed up with someone else. I'm just a bum."

She shook her head ever so little, and her eyes got deeper and blacker; and she took a deep breath like a swimmer going under water.

"Isn't it a pity, Joe, that you won't buy me—when

you're the only person I could possibly sell to?"

I've only got a little more to say about us, our marriage, and probably it isn't necessary.

What smells good in the store may stink in the stew pot. You can't blame a train for running on tracks. Ten years is a hell of a long time.

So, to get back to the present ...

10

When I went downstairs around ten the next morning, Elizabeth was in the living-room and old Andy Taylor was with her. I shook hands and asked Elizabeth why she hadn't called me.

"I wouldn't let her," said Andy. "Just stopped by for a little visit; nothing important. Have a good trip to the city?"

"So-so," I said.

"How'd you hurt your hand?"

"I cut it on a bottle I was opening," I said. "It's nothing serious."

He's a sharp old buzzard. A buzzard is just what he looks like, now that I come to think of it. He's got reddish-gray hair that's always hanging out from under his hat because he's too stingy to get it cut, and his nose is like a beak. I've never really seen his eyes they're so far back in his head. And I've never seen him in anything but an old broadcloth suit that you could beat from now until doomsday and not get the dust out of. He's somewhere past sixty. He lives in back of one of his buildings.

"Where's that hired girl of yours?" he shot out suddenly.

"What?" I said. "You mean Carol? Why, I guess she's—"

"I let her have a few days off," said Elizabeth. "The child's not been anywhere or got to do anything since she's been here."

"Saw her down to the bus station. Wondered where she was goin'."

I laughed and lit a cigarette. "Don't tell me you didn't find out."

"Meanin' to, but it kind of slipped my mind." He grinned. He knows that everyone knows how he is, and he doesn't care. He's rich enough that he doesn't have to.

"Believe I'll take one of your cigarettes," he said.

I gave him one. Elizabeth excused herself and went out.

Andy sat puffing on his cigarette, puffing on it until I thought he was going to suck it down his throat. He didn't talk while he smoked. Just kept puffing until there wasn't anything left to puff.

"Well, what's on your mind, Andy?" I said, when he had dropped the butt on an ash tray. "Want some passes to the show? I'll leave them for you at the box office."

"Thank you, Joe," he said.

"I guess my customer liability falls due this month," I said. "I can give you a check now if you want it."

"Ain't no hurry, Joe. No hurry at all."

I started getting fidgety. Waiting isn't my long suit, and, anyway, I knew what he had on his mind. He'd never given up prodding me about it since it had happened.

"Don't want to rent me another show for a percentage of the gross, do you?" I asked.

"Well, no. Can't say as I do."

"Okay," I said, "I'm here listening. You can talk when you're ready."

"You did give me a raw deal, Joe. Now, you'll admit that, won't you?"

"Oh, sure," I said. "Just the kind you'd like to give me."

"No, I wouldn't, Joe. I'm pretty tight, maybe, but I never crooked anyone out of a penny yet."

"I didn't crook you. I outsmarted you."

"I wouldn't brag about it, Joe. It don't take much brains to outsmart a man who trusts you. There's another name for that."

"Hell," I said, "you brought it up. What do you want to do about it, anyway?"

"I'll leave it to you, Joe. Twenty-five dollars a month don't even pay taxes on that building. What do you think you ought to do?"

"Well, I told you before, Andy. I'll let you out of the lease if you want to remodel the building—change it into something besides a show house."

"Huh!" he grunted. "An' what would that cost?"

"Plenty," I said. "Enough so you couldn't ever afford to convert back into a show again, no matter what kind of deal was put up to you."

"That's your last word, Joe? You've made up your mind not to do anything?"

"Not a goddam thing." I nodded. "You ought to know that by this time. You don't need money, so I don't feel sorry for you. And there's no way I can be forced to pay you more than twenty-five a month."

"How about yourself, Joe?"

"How do you mean?"

"Don't you think you ought to do the right thing for your own sake?"

"You mean so my conscience won't hurt?" I laughed. "Don't kid me, Andy."

"No, that ain't what I mean." He scowled and got up. "But I don't reckon there's any use talking to you. You mark my word, Joe Wilmot. You better change your ways or—or—"

He turned and stamped out without finishing.

I went into the kitchen and poured a cup of coffee.

Elizabeth was having some coffee, too, and I tried to strike up a conversation with her. Because, after all, we *had* been married for ten years and we didn't have much time left to spend together.

But she wasn't having any, and I didn't care much. There wasn't anything girlish about her this morning. She looked plain damned old.

I drove into town yawning, wishing that the whole business was over so I could relax and get some rest.

I fished my mail out of the box office and read it in my car. It was the usual stuff. Confirmation of bookings, advertisements, a copy of the *Motion Picture Herald*. I put the other stuff in my pocket and opened the *Herald*.

There was a story in it I was following. Some exhibitor out in the western part of the state had filed suit against the major exchanges to compel them to supply him with pictures. That was two years ago and they were still hearing evidence in the case. My personal opinion was that he'd better turn his house into a shooting-gallery.

You just can't win against the exchanges. They've got too many loopholes on their side. Take substitutions, for example.

Every once in a while I'll get a picture I didn't book in place of the one I did. It has to be that way in a business where a highly perishable product has maybe a hundred other buyers.

It happens pretty seldom with me because I stand in well, and I'm an important exhibitor. But if I didn't and wasn't—well, see what I mean? I *could* get substitutes five times out of five. My advertising money would be wasted. My customers would never know for sure what I was showing.

In any small-city house a large part of the patronage comes from the farmers and surrounding villages. I can stand out in front of my house and count people from half a dozen smaller towns. And it's because I get the pictures ahead of the smaller places.

It's no more than fair because I've got a bigger and better house and I can pay more than the small town—*and* the exchanges are willing to give me preferred booking. If they weren't I'd probably have to close up. I'd hate to try to operate with every wide place in the road around me getting pictures before I did. Almost as bad as I'd hate to show in court why I was entitled to pull trade away from another showman.

Jimmie Nedry showed up around eleven, and we went inside. It was Thursday, and our Friday's product should have been in for screening. But it wasn't. I called home, and it hadn't been dropped off there, either.

I put in a call to the city, and got Jiggs Larrimore on the wire. Jiggs is manager of one of the little exchanges. I don't particularly need him, and he needs me bad.

"I guess there's been a little mix-up, Joe," he said. "I'll tell you what you'd better do. You just hold over the picture you've been playing, and we'll take care of anything extra you have to pay on the option."

"Yeah?" I said. "Now I'll tell you what you'd better

do. You'd better get that picture here to me and get it here pronto."

"Now, look, Joe—"

"It's for my Friday-Saturday show. You know I've got to have a Western on Friday and Saturday. The yokels won't go for anything else."

"But it's too late to—"

"Huh-uh. No, it isn't Jiggs," I said. "Craig City's got that picture advertised for today. They've been advertising it here in my home-town paper. You pull their print over to me, Jiggs. It doesn't make any difference in a town that big whether they play horse opera on the week-end or not."

"Well, now"—I could hear him gulp—"I don't believe we can do that, Joe."

"Why not? Because it's one of Sol Panzer's houses?"

"Well. After all—"

"Look," I said. "How many of those Panzpalace houses are you in? Sol gives you a spot whenever he feels like it, and that ain't often. I buy the block. You pull that pic over here, Jiggs. You get it here quick. If you don't I'll set out every one of your dates and sell you a roll of tickets besides."

Jiggs sighed. "I hear you talking, Joe. Here it comes."

I hung up, and turned to Jimmie Nedry. "I guess that'll show Mr. Big Time Panzer something," I said. "He'll do a little thinking before he runs any more ads in this town."

"Yeah," said Jimmie. "So what?"

I let it pass, and went on outside. I knew Jimmie was feeling low about his money troubles, and I'd thought it would cheer him up to hear Jiggs Larrimore catch hell. That's one reason I'd cracked down on Jiggs. But

Jimmie didn't react like he should have. He couldn't think about anything but his own worries.

The thought flashed through my mind for a second that maybe there was something more to that picture mix-up than Solly Panzer's trying to pull a fast one on me. And crazy as the idea was it made me shiver to think about it.

It was just one of those things that happen. It couldn't be anything else. I had the Barclay in a spot that no one could touch and everyone knew it.

Just the same, though, I couldn't help thinking, *Wouldn't that be hell? Wouldn't it just be sweet to mix yourself in a murder and then find out that it hadn't got you anything?*

11

I worked my way around the square, shaking hands and slapping backs, and talking about crops and kids until I got to Sim's Pool Hall. Then I went inside and drank a bottle of beer and bought one for Sim. There were a lot of young bucks in there, and it wasn't long before most of them were around me. I'd picked up some new stories on film row. After we'd all had a few laughs and they'd bought me a beer or two I moved on again. Well, I did buy a package of mints, first.

About a block down the street I ran into Reverend Connors, the Christian Church minister. I bought a couple of tickets he was selling to a pie sociable, and wrote him out a pass to the show. I knew he wouldn't use it, and no one else could since I'd put his name on it.

"I'll tell you what, Reverend," I said. "If the church ladies would like to set up a table for their stuff in the lobby of the show I'd be glad to have them."

"Bless you, Brother Wilmot!" he said. "They'll be delighted to hear that."

He went away real pleased. I was sort of pleased myself. It would help to draw a crowd, and wherever there's a crowd there's business.

A half hour or so later I ran into Jeffery Higginbotham, the high school principal. He and I don't ever get familiar but we understand each other. He was kind of worried—on my account. The junior class was giving a play next month. They'd picked a Saturday night date to give it. What did I think?

Naturally, I thought it was a hell of a note, but I didn't say so.

"Why, that's swell," I said. "I'll let you have the show to put it on in."

"But we couldn't do that," he said. "You couldn't lose your night's business for us, Mr. Wilmot."

"I couldn't afford to, but I would," I said, "if it wasn't for sentiment among the town businessmen. You know, a picture show draws a lot of business to a town. I'm afraid they wouldn't like it if I didn't run on a Saturday night."

"No, I don't suppose they would," he said. "But—"

"Now, here's my idea," I said. "I'll turn the show over to you after midnight. The kids will love that. You know—having a regular midnight show, big-city style. And you'll catch a lot of customers you'd miss otherwise. A lot of people that come for the picture will stay to see the play."

"That's good reasoning," he said, and his eyes twinkled. "And a lot of people who intend to see the play will come early to see the picture. Or had you thought of that?"

"It never entered my mind," I said.

We both laughed, and I moved on again. I got back to the show at two o'clock when the matinee was starting.

Mrs. Artie Fletcher, my cashier—yes, and president of the Legion auxiliary—was talking over the telephone with her back half turned to the window. I've got a sign on that phone saying *No Personal Calls Please,* and I've given her more than one hint about using it. But it don't bother her any. I guess she thinks the rules don't apply to auxiliary women.

I guess they don't, either.

Several people had to wait around for tickets.

My doorman is Harry Clinkscales, the captain of the high school football team. If I could buy him for what he's worth and sell him for what he thinks he is I'd retire tomorrow. He's not even honest like you'd ordinarily expect a big overgrown pie-faced dumbbell to be. I know he knocks down on the popcorn machine, and if I didn't keep close watch on him he'd pass in a dozen females a day.

I wouldn't mind if it was just a few.

The day went fast. It was five o'clock before I knew it. I ate supper at the Palace Restaurant, had some pie and coffee at Mike's Barbecue, and bought some cigarettes at the City Drug.

I suppose that sounds pretty narrow and scheming, that trade-spreading stunt and some of the others I've told you about. But when everyone else is the same what choice have you got?

Bower—the guy that used to own the other house— couldn't be bothered about stuff like that. But look what happened to him. Elizabeth couldn't be bothered, either, and look at the shape she was in when I first met her.

I didn't tell you, I guess, but Elizabeth went into the show business in the first place because she knew she wasn't a mixer and she thought it was one business where she wouldn't have to be. People would just lay their money down quietly, and pass inside, and that would finish the transaction.

She thought!

At six o'clock I gave Jimmie Nedry a two-hour relief. After that, I went back outside.

Sheriff Rufe Waters and his deputy, Randy Cobb, sauntered up and stood beside me at the curb.

"Good show, Joe?" Rufe said.

"Fair," I said.

"Ain't got an empty seat or two you ain't using?" said Randy.

"Sure, I have," I said, and I gave the doorman the nod. "You boys go on in."

It wasn't more than fifteen minutes before Web Clay, our county attorney, showed up with his wife; and I had to pass them in, too. And before the evening was over I must have walked in a dozen.

Hell, I don't know how people get that way. I don't know what they're thinking about. Sure, I've got empty seats. That's the only kind I can sell. What if I walked into a bank and asked 'em if they had some four-bit pieces they weren't using.

It's the same proposition.

The Literary Club brought an author here once, and I was sold a ticket so I went to hear him. He was a big gawky guy named Thomas or Thompson or something like that, and I guess he'd put a few under his belt because he sure pulled all the stops.

He spent most of his time talking about people who asked him for free books and seemed to think he ought to be tickled to death to give 'em away. He said that sarcasm was wasted on such people and that the homicide laws ought to be amended to take care of them. Well, there wasn't a person in the house that hadn't hit me for an Annie Oakley at one time or another. But do you know what? Instead of getting mad or ashamed, they sat there and clapped their hands off. They didn't seem to realize that they were the kind of people this author was talking about.

Well . . .

At ten-thirty, Mrs. Artie Fletcher closed her window so fast she almost took off a customer's fingers; and Harry Clinkscales tore off without even pulling the switch on the popcorn machine.

I took a look inside. Jimmie Nedry was just making one of his perfect change-overs, and his daughter Lottie, my usher, was brushing up the aisles. I went back outside again. I didn't need to worry about those two. They'd be on the job as long as there was a customer in the house, and everything would be in good shape when they left.

I went into the box office, checked the receipts, and locked them in the floor safe. Just before midnight while I was taking a last turn through the house, Jimmie's two boys came in with what was left of the display matter. They'd been on the run all day, and they were shaking and so out of breath they could hardly talk. They hurried right on home with Lottie to get supper ready before Jimmie got there.

All of a sudden it hit me that the only people who were dependable and hard working were those that didn't amount to anything. It wasn't fair, but it was that way. And I wondered why it was.

I wondered why, when there was so damned many of 'em, they didn't get together and run things themselves. And I made up my mind if they ever did get an organization—a going organization, that is—they could count me in!

Elizabeth woke me up early Saturday morning.

"The film truck just came, Joe," she said. "It's here."

" 'Jeopardy of the Jungle'?"

"Yes. You'd better get up right away. We've got a lot to do."

I said okay, and she left the room. I didn't want to get up. I wanted to stay right there and leave everything that was going to happen a good long way in the future. And I couldn't. I couldn't because, while I didn't want to go through with it, I didn't want *not* to, either. That sounds crazy but it's the only way I know to put it.

Just a few days before, any little thing was enough to make me throw the brakes on. Like, for instance, passing up that hitchhiker. But now I knew nothing could stop me. I hadn't liked the scheme, but neither had I fought it. I'd just rocked along with it, getting a little more used to it every minute, and now it was doing the rocking.

I couldn't back out.

I didn't want to back out.

Coming out of the bathroom, I glanced into Elizabeth's room. A hat with a heavy veil was laying-lying—on a chair near the bed. Next to it was a little overnight bag. The hat was an old one and would never be missed in case anyone should get funny ideas and start checking up. The few odds and ends she was taking in the bag would never be missed, either.

I went downstairs, swallowed some coffee, and went out to the garage.

I'd got a travelogue, a newsreel, and a cartoon along with 'Jeopardy.' In all there were twenty-three reels of film.

"I was just thinking," I said. "Carol may not be able to get anyone. Perhaps we ought to wait until—"

"How are you going to wait?" Elizabeth asked. "You've got to go into the city."

"I don't have to," I said.

"Yes, you do, Joe. The farther you're away from things the better off it'll be. If Carol shouldn't get anyone there's no harm done. I'll straighten things up and we'll try again in a few weeks."

"But someone might look in and—"

"Don't be silly. I'll keep the door locked."

We ran the reels through the rewind to shake the water off of them. It was turned on full speed, since we weren't checking the film, and it didn't take long.

I unreeled fifteen or twenty feet of the cartoon, and Elizabeth knitted it back and forth through the other film. We shoved the pile underneath the rewind table.

I pulled the good cord loose from its connections, and hooked the motor up with the old one. I threw a few loops around it with the cartoon and pulled the rest of the reel under the table.

I stood back and looked things over.

The film was touching the bare copper of the cord in a couple of places. I shifted it back and forth until it was just right. Carol wouldn't need more than a minute. But she'd sure as hell need that.

Elizabeth was sitting on the stool. She looked even paler than usual.

"You didn't need to help with this," I said. "I could have done it."

She got up. "You're all through now? You're not going to leave that other cord on the floor are you?"

"Why not? It's the best way of getting rid of it."

"Yes," she said. And I wasn't just imagining that she was paler then.

She went out the door ahead of me. I put the padlock on it, and gave her the key.

That's the way it was. We'd done it so often in our minds that I guess it would have seemed stranger not doing it than doing it.

I went up to my room, threw a few things into my grip, and came back downstairs. Elizabeth got up from a chair in the living-room and took a step toward me. I took one toward her.

"Well, Joe?" she said.

"Well," I said. "I guess this is it. I guess we won't be seeing each other any more. That is, if Carol gets the—her party."

"She'll get her, all right," said Elizabeth. "I've never had any doubt about that."

"Well, good-by," I said. "I'll always remember you, Elizabeth."

"You'd better, Joe."

"I'll—What do you mean?"

"Twenty-five thousand dollars."

"That's what we agreed on," I said. "Where's the argument?"

I hoped she wouldn't say anything more. It's hell to want to sock your wife the last time you're seeing her.

"I want to make myself clear, Joe. If your memory should fail you there will be exceedingly unpleasant consequences."

"Hell," I said, "what do you think I am, anyway?"
"Exactly what I always did."
I walked out.

Ordinarily, if I'd wanted to go into the city I wouldn't have bothered to make excuses to anyone. I'd have just gone. But now it was different. I had to have a good reason for going, and there was only one I could think of.

I beat Jimmie Nedry to the show by about thirty minutes, and went up to the projection booth. By the time he got there I'd taken the parts cabinet off the wall and had everything in it spread out on the rewind table.

He didn't say anything at first, just gave me that sullen, hopeless look he'd been pulling lately, and stripped out of his coat, shirt, and undershirt. Those carbon arcs really heat up the booth. I went on pawing, though, and finally he asked me what I was looking for.

"I'm looking for the spare photoelectric cells for our sound heads," I said. "It doesn't look like we have any."

"We've got 'em," he grunted.

"Well, I don't believe we have, Jimmie," I said. "I thought I'd make a check on our parts last night when you were on your relief, and I couldn't find them then. And I've taken everything out this morning, and—"

"They got to be there," he said. "Let me look." He began sorting through the stuff impatiently, half sore. He wound up by picking up each part separately and putting it back in the cabinet. His face had fallen about a foot.

"I—I just can't believe it, Mr. Wilmot. We had some spares up there, well, I know it couldn't have been more than two or three days ago."

"You haven't used any since?"

"Of course I ain't! If I had I'd have told you so you could reorder."

"Hmmm," I said. "Did you actually see the cells or just the little carton they come in?"

"Well—"

"That's it," I said. "At one time or another we've replaced the cells in the machines and put the empty cartons back in the cabinet. I'm not saying you did it. I may have myself."

"But what became of the cartons?"

"They must have dropped down and got swept out. No one would pay any attention to them as long as they were empty."

"Yeah, but—"

"I'm not blaming you, Jimmie. The thing is to get some more. We don't want to be playing silent over Sunday."

"No," he nodded, "that would be bad. You'll bring some cells back when you go into the city?"

"I wasn't planning on going into the city," I said, "but I'll have to now. It's too late for the express to reach us, and the stores will be closed tomorrow."

"Yeah—I see." He rubbed his chin, giving me a puzzled, funny look. "When'll you be back?"

"Just as soon as I get the cells. Probably early tomorrow morning."

"You—you won't have to stay over for anything else?"

"Why should I?"

"Nothin'," he mumbled, turning around to the projectors. "I was just wondering."

A hundred miles up the road I stopped at a restaurant for a bite to eat, and called Carol from a booth phone.

She must have been waiting right by the phone because she answered right away.

"I'm coming in," I said. "Will I get to see you?"

She said, "No. I'm leaving right away."

That was right. It was what she was supposed to say.

"Get your baggage taken care of?"

"Not *all* of it," she said. "I'll send for the rest later."

That was right, too.

"Did you get in touch with that party you spoke about?"

"Yes. And she's going to be very helpful."

"Well, have a good trip," I said. "And be careful."

"I will be. You be careful," she said.

We said good-by and hung up.

13

The car was running pretty hot by the time I got to the city, and I had good reason to take it to a garage. I told them I wanted the radiator back-flushed, a grease job, and an oil change. They were rushed, since it was Saturday, and they wouldn't promise to get the work done before nine that night. I groused a little about it, but I left the car.

Of course, if I'd started back home right away I couldn't have got there ahead of Carol. But I didn't want to be on the road when things popped. I wanted to be able to prove where I was.

I bought two photoelectric cells at the theatrical equipment house, and dropped them into the first trash can I passed. It was just like throwing twelve bucks away, but it couldn't be helped. I'd left the two I'd lifted from the show in the car, and there was no way I could explain the extras. And, anyway, what was twelve bucks?

I could prove that I'd had to come into the city, and that I'd actually bought the cells. Twelve dollars was pretty cheap for that.

I ate dinner at a restaurant on film row, and walked around awhile, restless, not knowing what to do with myself. All the exchanges except Hap Chance's had been closed since noon, and I wasn't sure that I wanted to kill any time with him. On the other hand, a sharpie like that might be just the kind to use for an alibi.

I stopped across the street from his place, trying to decide whether to drop in on him, and he looked out and saw me. He got up, dimmed the lights and drew the shades. I was thinking, *What the hell?* when he opened the door and motioned.

I crossed the street. "What's up, Hap?" I said.

"Pop in, laddie," he said, "I'll tell you in a sec."

He closed the door and locked it, and we went back to his desk. He brought out the whisky and a couple of glasses, and we both had a drink. He poured a second for himself.

"Well, Hap?" I said.

"I've got some information for you, old man. I wouldn't care to have anyone know it came from me."

"All right," I said. "Under the hat."

"You recall our conversation of a few days ago?"

"Yes."

"What did you make of it?"

"Why," I said, "I hadn't thought much about it. I supposed, maybe, you had a buyer for a house and you thought you might make a deal for mine."

"Nothing else?"

"No."

He frowned slightly, shaking his head. "I suppose not. I didn't give you a great deal to go on. Still, there at the last, when you forgot to buy paper on 'Jep—'"

"I don't claim a perfect memory. What's on your mind, Hap?"

"You're broke, laddie."

"What?" I said.

"I say you're stony. I'd have told you the other

night, but I wasn't too sure about my facts. At any rate, I don't know that there's anything you could have done about it."

"You haven't told me anything yet," I said. "What do you mean I'm broke?"

"Sol Panzer's moving in on you."

I laughed. "Nuts, Hap."

"All right, laddie."

"The town's too small for Panzpalace. It isn't a fourth big enough."

"It's big enough," said Hap. "It's big enough if Sol says it is. Think it over. In ten years you've built a fine house with a fine business out of nothing. Sol can point to that if he needs to justify himself, which he won't. Panzer owns control of Panzpalace. He's always made money for the stockholders. Now—"

"I don't give a damn about that," I said. "Panzpalace doesn't build anything less than a million-dollar house, and a million-dollar house just won't pay off there."

"You mean you can't sell enough admissions?"

"Certainly that's what I mean. How else could you make it pay?"

"Oh, laddie"—Hap made a clicking noise with his tongue—"what hour yesterday were you born? You can make it pay by cutting your overhead, rather, by shifting the costs. *You* can't do it because you don't have any place to shift them to. But Sol has ninety-three other houses. He can make a house earn just as much or just as little as he wants it to."

"Yeah, but—but why does he want to do it?"

"I dropped you a hint about that the other night. I asked you if there was a chance that your house would be worth a million—meaning, of course, would anyone be jailed for paying you that much for it. I thought we might peddle it to him."

"Did you try?"

"No use. Merely wishful thinking on my part. There's a lot of loose change when you start breaking up a million dollars, but you have to break it to get it. Sol has to build. I saw that as soon as I'd taken time to study the matter."

I began to tremble inside. I mopped my face.

"You're not lying to me, Hap?"

"Really, old man—But I can't blame you for being disturbed. If you're looking for confirmation, drop around to the exchanges and try to buy for next season. I think you'll find that they'll stall you."

"Jesus!" I said.

"Or have they already?"

"I see it was a stall, now," I said. "I didn't think anything of it at the time. It's such a relief not to have them trying to load you that I—"

Hap clicked his tongue again, trying to look sympathetic. I saw his angle. Sol hadn't needed his stuff to shut me out. The other exchanges were enough. Now, since it wasn't costing him anything, Hap was palling up to me, hoping that it would hurt Panzer in some way.

"I can't tell you how sorry I am, old man. I was just wondering—"

"Yeah?" I said.

"Perhaps you could force Sol to drive a deal with you. You can probably pick up a dozen pix or so from the little fellows, and of course you can count on my line-up. Every last picture I've got. Why—"

"What the hell are you talking about?" I said. "If there was any way I could run on your stuff it wouldn't be open. And you wouldn't be sitting there offering it to me."

"Please, laddie. Not so loud."

"Nuts," I said. "Panzer tried to play without you and you found out about it. You don't care whether he finds out you told me. You hope he will. It'll teach him to call you in the next time he cuts a pie."

Hap sighed. "We should have been partners. Great minds, et cetera. You know what I thought when I first saw you tonight?"

"I don't particularly give a damn."

"Don't be rude, Joseph. I might slap the unholy God out of you."

"All right," I said. "What did you think?"

"Well, I thought you *had* caught my hint after all; that that was why you were in town."

"I don't get you," I said. "I had to come in to buy some photoelectric cells."

"Perfect," he beamed. "But let's not be coy with one another. You know my attitude toward insurance companies. Feel it's more or less a civic duty to rook 'em."

"Now, wait a minute," I said. "I—I—"

"I thought, here's old Joe, virtually on the point of losing his shirt, and here's this unwholesome insurance policy, just lying around and collecting dust and doing no one the slightest good. And I put myself in your place, laddie. I thought, now what would a keen chap like old Joseph do?"

"B-But—"

"You do have insurance on the show?"

"Certainly, I have. But, goddamit—"

"Don't be vehement, laddie. I'm on your side."

"Yeah," I said. "Yeah, but—*but*—" My voice rose, and he frowned and started to call me down. And then his eyes narrowed, and he just sat there watching me. It wasn't necessary to tell me to shut up. I couldn't say anything. I couldn't move.

You see? He had the whole thing wrong, and yet he was in the right. He was right enough to pin my ears back and keep them pinned, if he wanted to. And he would want to. He'd play it for all it was worth.

But, bad as that was, it wasn't what really got me. What got me, what made me feel like I was going crazy, was the realization that the woman was going to die for nothing. Her death wasn't going to mean a thing. It was just murder, nothing more than murder, with none of us better off than if she had lived.

And now there wasn't any way I could stop it. I knew those bus schedules backward and forward; and I knew it was too late.

There's nothing quite so silent as film row on Saturday night. The Playgrand exchange was half a dozen doors up the street, but when their phones began ringing they sounded like they were in the next room.

They stopped ringing in Playgrand and began in Utopian. And then they rang in Colfax and Wolfe. And finally—

Hap was watching me like a hawk. He spit on the carpet without ever taking his eyes off me, and picked up his phone.

"Yes," he said. "Righto, operator. Put 'em on . . . Mr. Wilmot? Why, yes. I believe I can reach him. Was there some message you—"

"Give me that phone," I said, and grabbed for it.

He planted his foot in my stomach, and I doubled up with the wind knocked out of me.

"What?" he said. "Why, that's terrible! I can't tell you how sorry I—Certainly, I will! Certainly. As a matter of fact, he's just stepped into the office. I'll break the news to him gently."

He hung up the receiver, poured a glassful of whisky, and handed it to me.

"Brace yourself, old man. There's been a terrible accident. Your wife—"

There was a grin on his face a foot wide.

14

All Stoneville is grieving over the death of Elizabeth Barclay Wilmot, wife of Joseph J. Wilmot, local theater magnate, who passed away in a fire at the Wilmot estate Saturday night. Cause of the fire has not been determined, but it is suspected that rats gnawing at the wiring may have been responsible. The fire broke out about nine o'clock, shortly after Mrs. Wilmot had returned from Wheat City where she had gone to pick up Miss Carol Farmer, a household employee. Miss Farmer, who was on her way back to Stoneville from a vacation, had missed her bus while dining in Wheat City, and had called Mrs. Wilmot to come after her. Upon reaching the Wilmot residence here, Miss Farmer went into the house and Mrs. Wilmot repaired to the upstairs of the garage, which was equipped as a film-inspecting room. When the fire burst into being a few minutes later, Miss Farmer notified the Stoneville fire department which promptly and efficiently answered the call. But little if anything could be done to defeat the holocaust. While the inspection room itself was fireproof, the heat was so intense that the supports and exterior walls of the building ignited and crumbled. Mrs. Wilmot was pinned beneath a work bench. Mr. Wilmot, who was out of town on business, was notified of the tragedy by telephone. Suffering from

shock and grief, he was accompanied home by Mr.
Harbert A. Chance, film company executive. Mr. Chance,
an old friend of Mr. Wilmot's will remain in Stoneville
temporarily to assist in the conduct of the latter's affairs.
Mr. Wilmot has been convalescing in the Stoneville
Sanitarium, suffering from shock and grief, but is
expected to . . .

I read a story one time about a fellow that was
accidentally slipped into a big job; president of a
company or something like that. He looked like the
guy that actually was president, see, and when this
guy ran off or fell in a mudhole or something and
wasn't ever seen again, why this one hooked his place.
He didn't know beans about the business, and all he
planned on doing was to stick around long enough to
snap a few rubber checks and maybe get the other
guy's gal alone in the parlor for a while. But once he
got inside, the graft looked so good that he decided to
stay for a real milking. He was scared out of his pants,
naturally, because he didn't know any more about the
setup than a hog does about ice skates. But he ran a
bluff, and damned if he didn't make good on it.
His work was just cut out for him, see what I mean?
The stenographers would bring him letters to sign,
and he'd just sign 'em. And when he got any letters,
his vice-presidents or some of his secretaries would
take charge of them. And when people showed up for
conferences all he had to do was keep his eyes and ears
open, and he could see what he had to do. He didn't
have to move. He *got* moved. As I remember the yarn,
he wound up by getting made president of a lot of
other companies and marrying the other guy's gal,
and no one ever knew the difference.
Well, when I read that I thought it was strictly off

the cob. And I knew it'd be just my luck to have the thing made into a movie and I'd have to see it. But if you asked me now I'd say it wasn't corn. If I hadn't been worried about Hap Chance, and being broke, I wouldn't have done much worrying. Up to a certain point.

I didn't have to explain the accident—if you want to call it that. There were several stories going around that were better than any I could dream up. I didn't have to pretend I was suffering from shock and grief. They told me I was.

A delegation brought me some mourning clothes Tuesday afternoon, and Sheriff Rufe Waters and County Attorney Web Clay and a couple of fellows from the chamber of commerce drove me over to the mortuary in a limousine. Rufe and Webb took me into the chapel to look at the casket—but not inside it— and then they took me right out again.

I didn't hear much of the services because someone thought I was looking peaked, and they took me into the rest room. They gave me a couple of drinks to brace me up, and made me lie down on the lounge. And after the services were over they got me up again.

I rode out to the cemetery with Rufe and Web and one of the Legion boys and a fellow from the Farmers' Union. Rufe is the wheel horse for the Democratic party and Web is the same for the Republicans. If I'd been picking a foursome to ride with from the standpoint of keeping all sides happy, I couldn't have done better. And I hadn't had to do it. It was done for me.

It started to rain a little on the edge of town, just a few drops, but by the time we passed our—my—place it was misting pretty hard. I looked up the lane toward the garage, and of course there wasn't any. Just part of the framework and a pile of timber and metal and ashes. But there was a guy chasing around, trying to cover things up with pieces of canvas.

I asked who he was.

"That's the investigator from the insurance company," said Rufe. "Looks like he'd have enough decency to lay off during the ceremony."

"I've got my eye on him," said Web. "I'm just hoping he gets out of line a little. He can't come into my county and tell me how to run things."

I wanted to ask him what the trouble was, but I decided it wouldn't be appropriate. Or smart. The longer I could stay in the background and let my friends do my arguing the better off I was.

I guess almost the whole county was at the cemetery. There wasn't room for half the people inside, and they were parked along the grade for almost a mile on either side of the gates.

They all stood up when we passed, stood along the side of the road or on their running-boards or wagon beds, with their heads bowed. It gave you an awfully funny feeling. It made you feel almost like it was Judgment Day; like they'd all been pulled up out of everywhere for the trumpet's blast before they could move. It was kind of scary.

I remember one woman in particular. She was standing up in a wagon box with a big fat squawling baby in each arm. They looked damned near as big as she was; and she'd started to feed them, I guess, because she had her blouse open and what babies go for was hanging out on each side. It wasn't hanging right, though, and the kids were as mad as all hell, twisting and screaming and grabbing at it, and trying to raise their heads up. But she just stood there with her head bowed like everyone else.

We drove through the cemetery gates, and got out. Web and Rufe stood by me at the grave.

The minister began his oratory; a lot of mumbo jumbo about being washed in the blood of the lamb and people being better off dead than they were alive; and all the time, by God, acting like it was deep stuff. And the different bands began to play "Nearer My God To Thee," and they couldn't play with themselves, let alone with each other. And the church choirs kept racing ahead and falling behind. And—but it wasn't funny. I've never felt more like bawling in my life.

There are some things so bad and so careless that you wish to God they didn't pretend to be good-intentioned so you could put in a holler without making a heel of yourself. I've felt pretty much the same way looking at newsreels of ceremonies at the tomb of the Unknown Soldier. The bands playing and the people singing, all in their own way, the right way; and the generals, the statesmen, and the club ladies all speaking a little piece for themselves. And they all mean so goddam well—I guess—and no one is responsible any more than I was responsible for her.

I bawled; there beside the grave with the rain coming down harder and harder. I felt just as bad as if I'd known the woman.

I could hardly see a thing I was crying so hard. I saw Carol for a second on the other side of the grave, and then everything got blurry again.

Web and Rufe led me away. We went back to the car and they put me inside while they waited outside, one at each door.

It came over me all of a sudden that I was a prisoner; that the reason they were with me was to watch me. I leaned forward to get out of the car, and Web Clay eased me back.

I tried it again. I knocked his hand out of the way.

"You let me out of here!" I yelled. "I can't stand any more! Take me away from here!"

"Maybe we'd better, Web," said Rufe. "Joe's been under an awful strain."

Web said, yes, I had, and went and got the other two fellows. We drove away.

Web rode with his arm around me, almost with my head pulled down against his chest; and Rufe made me take a new silk handkerchief to blow my nose on. They took me into the house.

"What you need, Joe, is a good stiff drink," said Web. "Rufe, you got anything in the car?"

"I've got something," I said, straightening up a little. "I guess we all need a little something."

We went up to my room and had a few good stiff drinks, and swapped a little talk. Rufe and Web got friendlier than I'd ever seen them. While we were up there, Carol and some of the town ladies were busy downstairs fixing coffee and laying out sandwiches and cake. When the crowd began to come in from the funeral, the boys took me downstairs again.

I was sat down and stood up and made to eat cake and sandwiches and coffee, and when the people began to file past me in a line on the way out, they— the ones that were taking care of me—even did my talking.

"Yes, yes. That's very kind of you, neighbor—"

"Joe appreciates that very much—"

"Joe thanks you very much—"

I guess they would have even shook—shaken— hands for me if they could have.

By this time it was dark, practically everyone was gone except the ladies who were staying to help Carol. I went upstairs and had a few more drinks and tried not to think. It was raining to beat hell now, and the wind was coming up. I heard Rufe and Web pulling out for town, and pretty soon another car left behind theirs. The insurance man's.

There seemed to be a draft coming from somewhere. I thought maybe someone had left a window open. I took another stiff drink and looked through the upstairs room by room. There wasn't any window open. I went downstairs again.

All the ladies had left except Mrs. Reverend Whitcomb. She was staying that night to keep the proprieties. She fussed around me for almost an hour, trying to do things for me that I didn't want done. When she'd worn us both out she hobbled into the downstairs bedroom and closed the door. I'd think she weighed around two-eighty. And she wasn't much taller than a quart of beer. She'd been going through doors sideways for so long that she kind of waltzed when she walked.

When she got into bed one of the slats popped like a gun going off. Then, there was a rasping, grating sound, like a bale of wire being dragged across a tin roof, and the whole house shook.

"Are you all right, Mrs. Whitcomb?" I called.

She was silent, or not exactly silent, either; I could hear her panting for breath.

"Quite all right, Brother Wilmot," she said finally.

I hesitated. "Are you sure there's nothing I can do for you?"

I knew damned well the bed had broken down.

"Oh, no, Brother Wilmot. I'm just dandy. Now you run along."

Carol was still busy in the kitchen. I went upstairs, took another drink and went to bed.

I didn't hear her when she came up the stairs. She

opened the door and came in without turning the light
on; and in one of the dim flashes of lightning from the
storm I saw her pulling her dress off over her head.

"You shouldn't do that, Carol," I whispered.

"It's all right," she whispered back. "I peeked in at
Mrs. Reverend Whitcomb. She's sleeping down inside
the bedstead. The mattress and springs fell through
with her."

I grinned. I even laughed a little, quietly. It's funny
how you still laugh.

"You'd better go on, anyway, Carol," I said. "I've
got a chill, a pretty bad cold. You're liable to catch it."

"I won't face you," she said.

I was lying with my knees drawn up, my hands
under the pillow; taking up most of the bed.

She got in with her back to me; pushed back gently
until my knees came down. She pulled one of my arms
under her and the other over her, and folded them over
her breasts; and she held them there with her own
arms.

"Now, you'll be warm," she said. And pretty soon:
"You were just afraid, that's what made you cold. You
don't need to be afraid, Joe."

I didn't say anything, thinking, and she spoke
again.

"Do you love me?"

"Sure I love you."

"You've got to, Joe. You just got to. Maybe you don't
want to now, but it's too late to change. You got to love
me."

"Hell," I said, "what are you talking about? I love
you or I wouldn't have done it, would I?"

She didn't answer right away, but I could feel her
getting ready. I knew, almost to a word, what she was
going to say. Because we weren't the same people any

more. If you won't stop at murder you won't stop at
lying or cheating or anything else.

"I don't know, Joe. Maybe—maybe you were afraid
of me, of what I might do. You and Elizabeth. Maybe
your business wasn't so good, and you thought—
well—"

"Carol! For God's sake—"

"I'm not saying it was that way. I'm—don't be mad
at me, Joe! I've had to—most everything I've had to do
and I've got to talk! I want to talk so you can tell me
I'm wrong!"

"Well, you're wrong," I said.

And I thought, *Jesus, what a break, what if I'd told
her about Hap and Panzer and the show being washed
up?* And I thought, *I'll have to get things straightened
out. She's just dumb enough to—*

"You mustn't try to see Elizabeth, Joe. You won't,
will you?"

"Of course I won't. Why should I?"

"You mustn't. You're mine now. You're all I've
got."

"All right," I said.

"You won't try to see her or write to her or
anything? Promise me, Joe. Please, Joe."

"For Pete's sake! All right, I promise!"

"You'll let me send the insurance money to her to
the General Delivery address like we agreed?"

"Yes. When I get it."

We went on talking, whispering in the darkness,
with the lightning staggering dully through the
windows and the rain scratching against the shingles
and splashing into the gutter. Everything had gone all
right, she said. The woman didn't have any friends or
relatives. They'd had separate seats on the bus. She
was practically the same size and coloring as Elizabeth.

Carol had told her that they were going on from
Wheat City by car—that they'd have to wait until a
friend from out in the country brought it in to them.
And the woman may have thought it was funny, but
she didn't say anything.

They met Elizabeth on a side street, and Elizabeth
got out and kept right on going. And Carol and the
woman drove home, and Carol took her up to the
garage to show her her quarters—

"Don't tell me any more," I said. "I don't want to
hear about it."

"All right," said Carol.

"I'm sorry," I said. "I meant, I don't want you to
talk about it. I know how hard it was on you."

There wasn't much said after that.

After a while Carol got up and locked the door and
set the alarm clock.

15

Appleton, the man from the insurance company, was already outside the next morning when I went downstairs. I walked over by the place where the garage had been and introduced myself.

He was a big fellow, not much over thirty, and he had a rather joking manner of speaking. When I came up he was bending over a sort of suitcase he had on the running-board of his coupé. One that opened at the top with a lot of vials and bottles and envelopes, and little racks and clips to hold them.

"I'm afraid there's not much to work on," I said, looking around.

"Oh, I've got everything I need already," he said. "I cleaned up the last of it yesterday evening. Just making a final check this morning."

"Did you—find anything to help you?" I asked.

"Don't know yet." He grinned. "I've got it all, though, up at the hotel. I've signed enough receipts for your county attorney to fill a bushel basket."

"I'm glad you've had co-operation," I said. "If there's anything I can do let me know."

"Swell," he said, "just pass the word along to the C.A. and the sheriff and their cohorts that the quicker I'm satisifed the quicker you'll get your dough."

"I'm not in any particular hurry to get the money," I said.

"Oh, hell," he said, "we're all in a hurry to get the money. What's your opinion on the origin of the fire?"

"I don't know," I said. "According to the paper, rats—"

He threw back his head and laughed. "I'll bet that tied you in knots, didn't it? Would rats be in a metal-lined room? Wouldn't your wife have known if there were rats? And would she have put herself within a hundred yards of them?"

"I've not had any experiences with fires," I said. "What's your idea?"

"I've got a couple. One is that it was incendiary." He grinned, watching my face. "The other, that it was an accident."

"Well—"

"Pretty good, huh? All I've got to do is get rid of one of 'em, and I can hand you a check or have you slapped in the jug."

And before I could say anything, he laughed and clapped me on the back to show that he was joking.

"I'm sorry, Mr. Wilmot," he said. "I know how you must feel at a time like this, and I don't mean to be flippant. I see so much tragedy that I'm a little hardened to it. Don't pay any attention to me."

"That's all right," I said.

"I'll be frank with you, Joe—Mr. Wilmot—"

"Joe's okay."

"I'm kind of puzzled, Joe. Now, you didn't have any knob-and-tube wiring in here? It was all in conduit, right?"

"Sure. Just like it is in my show."

"What about the cord on the rewind motor?"

"It was all right. So far as I know."

He shook his head reproachfully. "You mean to say you're not sure?"

"Well, of course I'm sure," I said. "Mrs. Wilmot would have been sure, anyway. She'd been doing this for almost ten years. If there was anything wrong with the cord she'd have known it."

"It looks like she would have, Joe," he nodded. "She didn't smoke, I understand?"

"No, she didn't."

"Well, there you are," said Appleton. "Apparently there wasn't any cause for the fire. And yet there was a fire. You see why I'm puzzled, Joe?"

"Yeah," I said. "I see."

"How long did you say Mrs. Wilmot had been doing this sort of work?"

"Ten years or so. Almost ever since we were married."

"Why did she do it? Don't get me wrong. We're not denying liability."

"I suppose she did it because she wanted to."

"Just like that, huh?" He laughed.

"Yes."

"You screen your stuff before you play it, don't you? Running it through the rewind here didn't save any time or money."

"I wouldn't say that. Every once in a while she'd run across a reel that was wound backward or needed splicing, and—"

"But not very often. Not often enough to justify so much time and expense. It strikes me that this setup would have been more of a nuisance than anything else."

Well, it was. I couldn't deny it.

"Tell me. Did she do any other work connected with the show?"

"Yes. She did quite a bit. Worked on the books now and then. Made out the deposit slips. Things like that."

"Why?"

"Why?" I said. But I knew what he meant.

"Sure. From what I've learned of you, Joe, you didn't need that kind of help. You're a first-rate businessman. I happen to know that Mrs. Wilmot was anything but an expert businesswoman."

"I don't see what that has to do with the fire."

"Maybe it hasn't got anything to do with it." He was still grinning, but his eyes were hard. "For twenty-five thousand bucks I could even ask foolish questions."

"I think I see what you're driving at," I said slowly. "You're implying that my wife was butting in where she wasn't wanted and that I resented it."

"Well, Joe?"

I nodded. Something seemed to nod my head. And when I spoke it was as though someone were whispering the words to me. The right words.

"It's probably pretty hard for you to understand," I said. "You see, Mrs. Wilmot was quite a bit older than I was. We didn't have any children. I think she felt from the beginning that she wasn't pulling her weight in the partnership—"

He cleared his throat, sort of embarrassed like. I went on.

"Her work didn't help me," I said—I heard myself saying. "It was a nuisance. I've spent hours undoing some of the things she did; and I used to get impatient and bawl her out. But I guess I was always ashamed afterward. She was trying to make up for things—for the things she couldn't give me and felt that she should—

"I wish she was back here, now. She could turn the show into a bathhouse and I'd never say a word. Anyway—well, that's the way it was. She did butt in, and I resented it. But we understood each other in spite of everything. That's all I've got to say."

Appleton blew his nose. "I think—I—I understand the situation, Joe. I'm sorry if I put the wrong interpretation on it."

"You've got your job to do," I said.

"I'll be frank with you. We don't like the looks of these fires where everything is so completely destroyed. Now, this Farmer girl—" He lowered his voice. "She was the last person to see Mrs. Wilmot alive. How did they get along together?"

"Why, all right, I believe," I said. "I can tell you this much. If Elizabeth hadn't wanted her here, she wouldn't have stayed one minute."

He nodded again. "That jibes with my information."

"If I had the slightest idea that Carol—"

"Now, don't let me put ideas into your head," he said quickly. "I'm just groping in the dark."

I glanced at my watch.

"I've got to be getting into town pretty quick," I said. "I suppose you'll be around for a while?"

"Oh, sure. You'll be seeing a lot of me before we get this thing settled."

I knew he meant just what he said, nothing more. I'd sold myself to him as much as I could be sold under the circumstances. He'd swallowed everything I'd said about Elizabeth.

Carol was fixing some breakfast when I went into the house. I sat down at the kitchen table and waited, and I think I said something about the coffee smelling good. She didn't answer me or turn around. Pretty soon I saw her hand go up to her face.

I swore under my breath, and got up. The back door was closed and the shades were drawn. I went over and stood beside her.

"Now what?" I said.

"N-Nothing."

"Come on, spit it out!"

I guess I sounded pretty harsh, but I was nervous. I had things to make me nervous. She whirled, her eyes flashing.

"I heard what you said to him!"

"What I said to him?"

"Yes. About Elizabeth!"

I couldn't figure out what she meant for a minute. Then I said, "Well, for God's sake, what did you think I should say to him? That I hated her guts and was damned glad she was gone? That would have sounded good, wouldn't it?"

"N-No—You didn't really mean it, did you?"

"Of course I didn't mean it."

She wiped her eyes and tried to smile. I sat down on a chair and pulled her onto my lap.

"Look, Carol," I said, "you're going to have to get over this suspiciousness and jealousy. If you don't it'll crop up at the wrong time, and that'll be just too bad. Don't you see? If people thought there was anything between you and me it would give you a motive for Elizabeth's—for this woman's—death."

"I know," she said. "I'll behave, Joe."

"You've got to, Carol," I said. "If they ever get the idea that you or I wanted Elizabeth out of the way, they'll do an autopsy on that—on the remains. They'll do one to end all autopsies. They won't know what to look for so they'll look for everything. And they'll find out it wasn't Elizabeth."

"But—well, there wasn't anything left—"

"Oh, yes, there was. The teeth were left, and that's all they'd need. The teeth would show that it wasn't Elizabeth."

She didn't know about things like that. She sat looking at me, making sure I wasn't kidding.

"Maybe—You don't suppose they've already—"

"Not a chance," I said. "If they had we wouldn't be sitting here. Oh, sure, they've had an inquest. Decided she died by reason of fire and so on. But that's all they've done, and we mustn't give them any reason to do any more than that. You'd better clear out of here tomorrow, at the latest."

"No!" She threw her arms around my neck. "Please don't make me, Joe!"

"But you've got to, Carol. We planned it that way. It don't look right for us to be staying here together."

"No! I don't care how we planned. It's different now."

"You'll be all right. You can get you a little job of some kind here in town and go ahead to school. In six or seven months, when all this blows over, we can start seeing each other and—"

"But what if something should happen that I ought to know about? You wouldn't be able to let me know until—until it was too late."

"It'd be too late from the start," I said. "This isn't something we can run out on if things get hot. Anyway, if anything went wrong you'd know it as soon as I would."

"No, I wouldn't, Joe."

"Why the hell wouldn't you?"

"Elizabeth was your wife, and I was the last one to be seen with her. And you were out of town when it happened. They'd talk to you before they did anything."

"Well," I said, "what of it? You're not going to be at

the north pole. If talking to you would do any good after things had gone that far, I could reach you easily enough."

She sat not looking at me. "They can't prove anything against you, Joe," she said in a funny voice. "Not what they can with me. If—if I took the blame—"

"Oh," I said slowly. "I see."

"Please, Joe—"

"Why don't you say what you mean?" I said. "You think if I got the chance I'd throw everything on you. Is that it?"

I shoved her to her feet and got up, but before I could move away she had her arms around me. She began crying again, and her breasts shivered against me, and I patted her and finally held her close.

"You shouldn't feel that way, Carol," I said. "We've got to trust each other."

"I d-do, Joe!" she said. "I trust you and love you so much that—and that wasn't the reason I wanted to stay! I—I just want to be near you. It doesn't seem like I'm living when I'm not with you."

Well, hell. I was pretty sure she meant it, but even if she didn't it sounded good. A woman can't make a man sore talking like that.

"Well," I said, "we'll talk about it again. I guess it will be all right if you stay around a few days. Maybe something will turn up by that time."

"That Mr. Chance. How long is he going to be in town?"

"I don't know," I said, wishing to God that I did. "I've got a lot of stuff to catch up on. He may be around helping me for quite a while."

"If he stayed here, too, it'd be all right for me to stay, wouldn't it?"

I didn't know how to get around that one. If I'd had my way Hap would be staying at the bottom of some good deep well.

"We'll see," I said.

16

I told Carol I wasn't hungry yet and left the house without eating breakfast. If there was ever a time in my life that I needed to keep my mind clear this was it, so I got away before I could be caught up in another argument.

I stopped at the Elite Café and ordered ham an'; and while I was eating Web Clay came in for a cigar. He saw me and came back to my booth. He'd already eaten but I got him to take a cup of coffee.

"Web," I said, after we'd talked for a while, "what do you think about the fire? About Elizabeth's death?"

"I don't think you need to ask me that, Joe," he said. "She was an irreplaceable loss to the entire community. I grieved with you."

"I appreciate that, Web," I said. "What I'm asking is, do you think Elizabeth could have been murdered and that the fire was used to cover up the crime?"

A slow flush spread over his face. He lit his cigar and dropped the match into his coffee cup.

"You don't think my investigation of the case was sufficiently thorough?"

"Now, Web—"

"You're a friend, Joe. I knew—I believed—that you trusted me, and I wanted to spare you all the pain that

I could. Now, I'll tell you something; something that only Rufe and I have known up to now. Before that fire was cold, before that whippersnapper Appleton got here, I had a man here from the state bureau of criminal investigation. He went over the ground thoroughly, and found nothing of an incendiary character. It was his theory that the fire must have been started by rats."

"But—"

"I know. We don't see how it could have been. But if it wasn't for the impossible and improbable we wouldn't have any accidents. Do you recall reading, a few years back, about the hardware clerk who was killed while unpacking a shipment of rifles? The gun had never been out of the packing-case, but it was loaded. It *couldn't* have happened at the factory. The chief inspector had examined it and sealed the breach with his tag. It *couldn't* have happened at the store because it had never been out of the box. But it *did* happen, Joe."

"I remember the case," I said. "Well, suppose, then, that the fire was an accident—and I've felt like you that it must have been. But—"

"The two things go together, Joe. Elizabeth's death was undoubtedly caused by the fire. It's true that the post mortem, such as it was, was not very revealing. The body—excuse me, Joe—was pinned beneath the remains of that metal table and other wreckage. But we were able to ascertain that the fire and nothing but the fire caused her death. That's all we need to know."

"I see," I said.

"She actually died of the fire, Joe. Therefore, in the absence of any incendiary materials or mechanism, we know that her death was an accident."

"Yeah—yes," I said.

He spread his hands. "Well, you see, Joe? I didn't take the case as lightly as you seemed to think I did. I didn't go around with a lot of fuss and bluster—"

"Now, Web," I said. "I wasn't criticizing."

"That's all right. I know this man Appleton has got you all stirred up. We may as well talk the thing out now that we've started. When I say that the fire caused Elizabeth's death I'm not overlooking the possibility that she could have been stunned and left to die in the fire. You were going to ask me about that, weren't you?"

"Well," I said, "it did occur to me that—"

"But where is your motive, Joe? You've got to have a motive, haven't you? Now, you—excuse me—profited by the death. But you weren't there, and, as I've said, there was no trace of a delayed-mechanism device; tallow or anything of that kind. And there always is some trace where anything of the kind has been used. Could she have been the victim of robbery or assault by some person unknown? We know that she couldn't. There wasn't time for it. The fire broke out almost as soon as she got home.

"Then there's—what's her name?—Carol Farmer. She was the last to see Elizabeth alive, and she was on the grounds. But what do we find there? Why, she and Elizabeth were on the best of terms. Elizabeth had taken her in and given her work. She'd just treated her to a holiday. She'd driven all the way to Wheat City to bring her home.

"We're friends, Joe, but I've always put duty ahead of friendship. I even considered the possibility—ha, ha—the impossibility, I should say, that you were attracted to Miss Farmer. Ha, ha. I'd hate to go before a jury with a theory of that kind. One look at her, and they'd lock me up. They'd send for a strait jacket—ha, ha, ha!"

I laughed right along with him. I think I've already said that no one saw in Carol what I saw. It suited me fine if they never did.

He went on talking while I ate, working himself into a good humor. As we were leaving the place we ran into Rufe Waters. Appleton had been in to needle him about something or other, and he was hopping mad. He was threatening to punch him in the nose if he came near him again.

I told Web and Rufe so-long, and drove over to the show. I parked in front of Bower's old house, feeling fairly good. Appleton was getting nowhere fast. In a few days he'd probably decide to pay off and clear out.

I got out of the car and started across the street. Then something nailed to the box office of Bower's old place caught my eye, and I turned around and went up on the sidewalk. It was one of Andy Taylor signs. It said:

FOR RENT

Taylor Inv. & Ins. Co.

I was standing there staring at it, not knowing whether to laugh or get sore, when Andy came up. I guess he must have been standing a few doors down the street, waiting for me.

"What's the idea, Andy?" I said. "You know you can't rent this building. I've got it under lease."

"But not the right kind of lease, Joe." He waggled his head. "That twenty-five a month don't hardly pay my taxes."

"I can't help that. I—"

"How's your hand?"

"What?" I said. "Why, it's all right."

"Looks like a pretty bad burn. How'd you get it?"

"Oh, hell," I said, without thinking. "When you're working around motion-picture equipment you're liable to—"

"Got it over to the show, huh?"

"Where else would I get it? Now, dammit, Andy get that sign—"

"You could have got it up to your house. Out there in the garage. There could have been something wrong with the machinery out there. Somethin' that you let go without fixing an' that started the fire."

"And wouldn't that tickle you pink?" I said. But my heart began to beat faster.

"You didn't get that burn at the show, Joe."

"The hell I didn't!"

"Huh-uh. I saw you that night when you were hangin' out around the front of the Barclay, and you didn't have nothing wrong with your hand. But you did the next morning when I talked with you up at your house. Reckon you remember, all right. You told me then that you'd cut it on a bottle."

"Well," I said, "maybe I—" But what was the use lying about it? With my hand unwrapped anyone could see that it was a burn.

"Still want to take the sign down, Joe?"

I hesitated and shook my head. "To tell the truth, I don't care either way. If anyone wants to try to compete with the Barclay in this rattrap they can hop to it."

"I'll take it down."

"Suit yourself," I said.

"I'll take it down. I just wanted to see how you felt about things." He pulled the sign loose from its tacks and crumpled it, grinning. "I reckon you and me had better have a good long talk, Joe. Private."

"I'm busy," I said. "I've got a lot of business to catch up with."

"It ain't as important as mine. Think it over, Joe."

He let out a mean cackle and shuffled off down the street. And I let him go. I didn't give him the horse laugh or tell him to go to hell, as I should have. I couldn't. If you're a poker player you know what I mean.

You're holding, say, kings full in a big pot and everyone has laid down but you and one other guy, a guy with a big stack. And he gives your chips the once-over, counting 'em, and antes for exactly that amount. Well? You'd bet your right arm he couldn't beat your full house, but they're not taking right arms; just chips. And if you're wrong you're out of the game. So you lay down, and the other guy wins—with a pair of deuces.

I crossed over to the show and went up to the projection booth. Jimmie Nedry wasn't there and neither was Hap, and the booth was messy as hell. There was even a reel of film left in the right projector. I ran it out, rewound it, and put it in the film cabinet. Then I went back downstairs and looked up and down the street for Jimmie. Show business gets you that way. No matter what else you got on your mind, you can't forget the show.

Jimmie lived in a little dump over across the tracks, and he didn't have a telephone. I was wondering whether I should drive over and see what was up when he and Blair came around the corner in Blair's car. Blair pulled in a little toward the curb, and I went out to them.

"My deepest sympathy, Joe," he said. "I hope you received our floral offering."

"Yes, I did," I said. "Thanks very much, Blair."

"I was planning on bringing Jimmie and his wife to the obsequies, but they didn't feel that they should attend."

"Why? Why didn't you, Jimmie?" I said. "The show was closed. You didn't need an invitation."

"We didn't because we didn't have any decent clothes to wear, that's why!" Jimmie snarled.

"Well," I said, "I know you wanted to, anyway. It's the spirit that counts in these things."

Blair threw back his head and laughed.

"Good old Joe," he said. "Always right in there pitching, aren't you?"

"Somebody's got to," I said. "Are you coming in pretty soon, Jimmie? It's only about an hour until show time."

He shook his head without looking at me. "I'm takin' a couple weeks off."

"Huh?" I said.

"That's right, Joe." Blair leaned around him, grinning. "Mr. Chance is giving Jimmie a vacation—at full pay. Don't tell me you didn't know about it?"

"I didn't, but it's all right."

"Mr. Chance a partner of yours now?"

"Whatever he does is all right," I said. "He's been kind enough to take care of things for me. He'll probably have to stay on for a while longer."

"Well,"—Blair stroked his chin—"technically he doesn't have the owner's right to operate the projectors. But we'll play along with you. Under the circumstances."

"Thanks," I said.

"Don't mention it, Joe. You don't owe me a thing."

He laughed again, and Jimmie kind of smirked, and they drove off.

I headed for Hap's hotel, boiling.

He was in his room, dressing, when I went up. He had on his pants and shoes, and he came to the door taking the pins out of one of those fancy twenty-dollar shirts.

"Goddam you, Hap," I said. "What's the idea of giving Jimmie two weeks off? What do you think you've got on me, anyway? I suppose you think I'm going to pay him."

"Entirely unnecessary, old man. I paid him myself—out of the receipts."

"I asked you what the idea was!"

"Just a sec," he said. "I'll open the windows. They can hear us in the next block then as well as this one."

I sat down and lowered my voice. "All right. Spill it."

"Why, it's quite simple, laddie. I intend to stay around for a time, and staying requires some justification. Ergo, young James gets a rest; a rest which, even from my conservative viewpoint, seems long overdue."

"Generous, aren't you?" I said.

"Oh, now, but why shouldn't I be with your money?" He raised his eyebrows. "As a matter of fact, however, I'm quite taken with Jamie boy. He's the sort I've often found it profitable to cultivate. You know? The humble downtrodden worm with big ears?"

"If you intend to pump him about me," I said, "you won't get much."

"Probably not, probably not," he said. "You always were frightfully clever. And it isn't really necessary, is it? Still—"

"What do you want, Hap?"

"Ah, now that's being sensible." He sat down on the edge of the bed, and poked an arm into his shirt. "Shall we say about five thousand dollars?"

"What for? Why should I give you five grand?"

"Well, to put it euphemistically, we'll say it's for the replacement of sixteen reels of priceless film."

"Priceless? That crap!"

"Or we can say it's to keep me from doing my unpleasant duty. Unpleasant, that is, from the standpoint of losing five thousand. Aside from that, I really don't care whether you swing or not."

He lit a cigarette and held the match, watching a fly crawl across the scarf of the reading-table. Suddenly, his hand went out and he stabbed it through with a pin. He held it into the flame, turning it while it sputtered and frizzled. He dropped it onto the floor and smeared it with his foot.

"Dashed funny thing, fire, isn't it?"

"Hap," I said. "Hap, suppose I had known that Sol Panzer was moving in on me, that I was broke. If I was trying to—if I was taking a quick way out, I'd have fired the show. I carry sixty thousand straight on it, plus one-fifty a week operation loss."

"Uh-*hah*." He nodded. "Exactly the thought that occurred to me until I'd inspected your house. A splendid piece of construction, laddie. Utterly fireproof."

"But—but I didn't—"

"But me not buts, old man. Simply earmark five of the twenty-five thousand now due you as indemnity for your late spouse for yours truly. And please hurry it along. I'm purchasing a new car."

"I can't—there's no way I can hurry it," I said.

"No? I suppose not. Well, it shouldn't be long at any rate."

"Yeah, but—"

He looked at me sharply. "You haven't bungled things, have you?"

"No. I didn't mean that. Everything's jake."

"If I thought you were going to be turned up anyway—" He paused, frowning. "You know I have a very large conscience. I'm not at all sure that five thousand will be sufficient to salve it."

"Yeah," I said, "I know."

I'd been bluffed again. If I'd told him to go to hell in the beginning—But I couldn't tell him. Not any more than I could have told Andy Taylor to take his sign down. Now, as long as I had anything to get they'd never let up on me. And if either one of them got the idea that I might get the murder pinned on me, they'd step right in and give me a shove.

A person would be nuts to hold back evidence in a murder case unless he stood to clean up by it. There's such a thing as being an accessory. Besides, the insurance company would probably come through pretty heavy for information that would save twenty-five grand.

Hap finished dressing and we went downstairs together. I told him that I was running into the city.

"Oh?" he said. "You wouldn't be taking a powder on me, would you?"

"Do I look stupid!" I said. "Why should I?"

"No," he said, "I suppose you wouldn't. You want to check on my news about Panzer. Is that it?"

"I want to see if I can do something about it."

"Such as?"

"I don't know," I said. "But I've got to make an effort. I've got a hundred-thousand-dollar property here. I can't just sit back and let it slide without lifting a hand."

He stood studying me a moment, then nodded and opened the door of the car. He even took me by the elbow and made as if to help me in.

"Well, the best of luck to you, laddie, and Godspeed and all that rot."

"So long," I said.

"I have tremendous faith in you, old man. As well as a certain mercenary interest—you know?"

I drove off without answering. I knew, all right. He'd want a good heavy cut on anything I was able to pull. The more I had the more he and Andy would demand.

I eased up on the gas just outside of town, and started looking for a crossroads to turn around on. There wasn't a damned bit of use driving into the city. There wasn't any way I could stop Panzer, and even if there was what would it get me? It would all go for blackmail.

As I say, I almost stopped and turned around. And then I stepped on the gas and went on toward the city. But fast.

Carol? Well, sure, she wasn't to be overlooked and I hadn't. But as long as I could keep her from knowing I was skinned clean until afterward it would be all right. As long as she was sure I wasn't going to run out on her, she really wouldn't give a whoop about the money.

Believe it or not, it was Elizabeth who had slipped my mind. With Hap and Andy both tackling me in the space of an hour, Elizabeth had slipped into the background. And, anyway, it wouldn't have made much difference if she hadn't. Elizabeth was supposed to be dead. I couldn't tell Hap or Andy that the twenty-five grand had to go to her.

It would have to, though. What was it she'd said? *"There will be exceedingly unpleasant consequences if your memory should fail you—"*

She'd have to get it all, right up to the last penny.

Keeping Hap and Andy quiet wouldn't mean a thing, otherwise.

I had to go on. I had to keep the Barclay valuable so that I'd have something to trade for Hap's and Andy's silence.

With the best luck in the world I couldn't wind up with anything. With a little bad luck—just a little— well—

It wasn't right. It was crazy. All this trouble over a woman I didn't know—hadn't ever even seen; a woman, who, when you got right down to cases, didn't amount to a damn.

17

I woke up the next morning about six o'clock and just lay in bed, not knowing what to do, until after nine. In the back of my mind, I guess, I was trying to kid myself that Hap had been stringing me about Panzer. Or that, maybe, he'd had the wrong dope. And I hated to get up and find out the truth.

Finally, a little after nine, I got up, caught some breakfast and a barbershop shave, and headed for the row. I hadn't brought any toilet articles with me. I'd been afraid to bring any luggage on account of Carol. I was wondering now what kind of story I'd hand her when I got back.

Everyone on the row had heard about the fire, and I wasted about an hour shaking hands and receiving sympathy before I could get to the Utopian exchange. Of course there was more of the same stuff there. But the manager saw it was bothering me and he cut it short by taking me back into his office.

Maybe I told you he was an old friend of mine? I'd known him since the days when he was peddling film and I was hauling it.

We had a couple of drinks and talked a little. After a few minutes, he took out his watch and glanced at it.

"Well, Joe," he said, "what brings you into town? What's on your mind?"

"Not much of anything, Al," I said. "I just wanted to get away from things for a day or two."

"I see. I understand." He shuffled some papers on his desk. "Well, I'm glad you dropped in."

"I was just wondering," I said, "if you had anything on next season's product yet. Of course, I know you've always got a good line-up, but if you had anything unusual I'd kind of like to know. I've been figuring on enlarging the house a little."

He sat there, smiling and nodding. "I believe I have got a few press sheets, Joe. Yeah, here's something. Take at look at those. Something, huh? I'm not going to run down our competitors, but you can see for yourself that—that—"

His eyes met mine, and the sheets slid out of his hand. He cleared his throat, and looked away.

"You've got a nice house, Joe. It always struck me as being just about the right size."

"Thanks," I said.

I'd known it was coming, but it didn't make it any easier to take. I knew it was kid stuff, foolish, to argue. But I couldn't help myself.

"It always seemed to me, Al," I said, "that I was a white man to deal with. I don't give nothing away, but I don't ask for noth—anything. If I'm not profitable to deal with, that's a different matter. But it always seemed to me like I was."

"Oh, hell, Joe," he said. "I'm in the business so I've got to talk price, but I don't think you've actually skinned us six times in ten years. I wouldn't say that to everyone, but I'll say it to you. You're a hundred-percenter in my books."

"Well, that's the way I feel," I said. "You've maybe skinned me a few times on superspecials, and you've got a damned bad habit of accidentally shipping me stuff I don't want on the same invoice with stuff that I do, so that I have to take all or nothing. But when I look back upon our whole friendship it's been pretty pleasant. It's something I hate to see broken up. I mean if it was going to be broken up."

"I'm glad you said that, Joe. I like to keep things on a friendly basis. After all, what are we arguing about? It's just a hypothetical case."

"Sure," I said. "Oh, sure. But take even a hypothetical case, Al; it's kind of hard for me to understand. I mean, I think I get it but I'm not sure. The town isn't going to get a whole lot bigger, if any, and film rentals are based on population. A can of film is a can of film. If you push it too far back on the shelf it begins to stink. Twenty-five per cent more, and I could reach it. Fifty, and I'm still not crazy. They'll let me go around if I wear a muzzle. But higher than that—well, they call in the health department."

"They've called it in before, Joe."

"You know what I mean," I said.

"It's hard to understand, all right," he said. "Personally, I don't try to. I just sit back and take orders. By the way, have you seen 'Light o' Dawn' yet? We booked it into the Panzpalace here in town last week."

"I played it," I said. "Don't you remember how you jacked me from twenty-five to thirty bucks for it?"

He didn't seem to hear me.

"We booked it into Panzpalace at fifty per cent of the gross. It pulled seventeen grand the first five days."

I got up and held out my hand. "Well, good-by," I said. "I've got to go buy a bottle of liniment."

"Goddamit, Joe," he said, "I like you. If there's ever anything I can do for you—personally, that is—you know where to come."

"I don't think there's anything you can do, Al."

"Well—" He let me get to the door. "Come back a minute, Joe."

I went back and sat down.

"Joe, I feel like a heel about this."

"What for?" I said. "It's just a hypothetical case."

"Oh, can that crap. The cat's out of the bag. I feel terrible about it, Joe. It's a hell of a note to hit a man with a thing like this right after he's lost his wife."

"I won't argue with you there," I said. "It looks like if Sol had to build another house he could have picked some spot besides Stoneville."

"No, he couldn't, Joe." Al shook his head. "You've got the best show town in the state. You've got a draw there of a town three times its size. It's the only place where he could possibly justify the building of another Panzpalace."

"It's going to be one then? One of his regular articles?"

"It has to be, Joe. You've got a pretty nice house there yourself. Sol couldn't build enough house for three or four hundred grand, even a half million, to freeze you out."

"I don't know that I get you," I said.

"Sure, you do. You mentioned it yourself a few minutes ago. If you had to, you could pay three or four times as much for product as you are now and keep running. But you couldn't pay six or seven times as much. Neither could Sol with less than a million-buck house. I mean, he couldn't justify rentals like that."

"I see," I said. "But actually he won't pay you any more than I do, if he pays that much. He'll shave you down somewhere else in the chain."

Al shrugged. "I showed you the answer to that, Joe. Panzpalace controls every important house in the state—the big city houses that play product on percentage instead of at a flat rate. As long as he doesn't ask us to do anything out-and-out illegal we've got to play with him."

"I'll make you a little bet," I said. "I'll bet inside of ten-fifteen years Panzer has shaved you enough, you and the other exchanges, to pay for that house."

"Maybe. I just work here."

"You're cutting your own throats, Al!"

"Better worry about yourself, Joe. What are your plans?"

"I—I haven't thought too far ahead," I said.

"Why don't you go and see Sol? Maybe you could work out something. I happen to know he likes you."

"Yeah," I said, "he must."

"He does, Joe." Al leaned forward. "Look. Those big boys don't look on things like you and I do. The way Sol sees it, it don't make no difference if there's a Barclay in Stoneville or not. Relatively, you know. It's unimportant. But if he don't put in this Panzpalace— and like I say he's got to put it in Stoneville—he sees himself as losing several million dollars."

I let that sink in, and, if there'd been a laugh left in me, it would have come out.

"I see," I said. "It's easy for a man to figure that way. You lose track of the fact that something that doesn't mean a thing to you may mean a hell of a lot to the guy that has it."

"That's it exactly."

"But how does he figure several million dollars?"

"Well, Sol has a reputation as a money-maker, doesn't he? When he puts up a new house the public looks on it as another mint."

"They're not far wrong at that," I said. "I see. Panzpalace stock will take a jump."

"It will, but don't get any ideas, Joe. This is Sol's surprise and only he knows exactly when he's going to pull it. He'll drive the stock down first. If you got in anywhere besides the basement you'd lose your shirt."

"Not bad," I said.

"But that's only part of the picture, Joe." Al held up a finger. "A Panzpalace house will use around ten thousand dollars worth of paper and display matter a year. If you and I bought it, it'd mean a flat outlay of ten grand, but Sol uses the same paper over and over. And he owns his own paper company. It's not a big outfit; has a capitalization of about a quarter of a million. But—"

But that was all to the good. Dumping ten thousand bucks' profit into a company that size meant a four-percent increase in dividends.

"Then there's his film-express company. It'll take a jump in profits with practically no increase in overhead. And his equipment companies, Joe. You know what show-house equipment is; high-profit, slow-moving stuff. A big order suddenly dumped in on those companies—"

My head began to swim. I'd thought I was halfway smart but beside Panzer I wasn't anything. He'd mop up in a dozen different ways, and the mopping up would be legitimate. His companies *would* be worth more. He'd have an actual operating loss in Stoneville, but it wouldn't ever show, and the house wouldn't cost him anything in the long run. He could show that he was increasing Panzpalace assets by a million bucks. That would stop any squawks.

Of course, someone was going to lose. The money had to come from somewhere. Suckers would be shaken out. The film companies would have to pinch a little, and there'd be wage cuts and layoffs. The—But what the hell of it? Sol would mop up and he'd be in the clear.

That's business.

Al leaned back in his chair. "By the way, Joe, who tipped you off?"

"No one," I said. "I just had a premonition."

"I read the papers, Joe. Hap Chance seems to be your bosom friend all of a sudden. Well, all I got to say is I wouldn't want to be in his shoes. This is one time he's got out beyond his depth. I suppose he thought this was just a little petty chiseling that he should be taken in on."

I didn't answer him. I didn't want to talk about Hap. If he was washed up on the row—and Sol could wash him up if he wanted to take the trouble—he'd bear down that much harder on me.

"When's Sol moving in, Al?"

"Only Sol knows that."

"Where's he going to build?"

"Well—" He hesitated. "Maybe I've been talking too much. But you can figure it out for yourself. Where would you build if you were in his place?"

"That's simple," I said. "You couldn't pick a better show lot than the one I've got, and people are accustomed to going in that direction. But—but—"

I choked up. I could feel my face turning purple. Al looked down at his desk nervously.

"Now, Joe. You couldn't expect him to talk it over with you."

"Goddamit," I said. "I'll make him wish he had! Maybe I won't sell! Maybe I got some ideas on making money, myself! Maybe—"

"You won't have any income, Joe. How long do you think you can play holdout?"

"A hell of a lot longer than Sol thinks! I don't give a goddam if I starve, I'll—I'll—"

I choked up again. I wouldn't get a chance to starve. I wouldn't even have time to get real hungry before Hap or Andy or Elizabeth or—

"You see, Joe? It wouldn't be smart, would it?"

"No," I said, "it wouldn't be smart."

I got up and walked out.

18

I've probably given you the idea that Elizabeth didn't have much tact or, at least, that she didn't go out of her way to use it. And that's true and it was the cause of a lot of our trouble. But now that I think about it, it seems like the thing that caused the most hell was that I never knew quite how she was going to react to a given situation.

I don't mean that I'd want any woman to be all cut and dried in her actions, or that I ever expected anyone to use me as a pattern. But I do say you've got to have some—well, some standard of conduct or you don't have anything at all. You've got to know whether what you're going to do will make a person happy or sore. You've got to know whether a person is actually happy when they—he—she looks like and says she is or at least you've got to know that she isn't. And if that sounds mixed up I am and I was, right from the day we were married.

We closed the show up for two weeks for our honeymoon, since it wasn't making a damned thing anyway; and, seeing that it was summer, we went to a resort up in the eastern part of the state. It was just a small place—but nothing cheap by a long shot—and everyone had you sized up the minute you walked in. Everyone knew that Elizabeth and I were just married, and everyone was doing a little under-the-breath kidding about it. And I thought that Elizabeth was taking it perfectly all right—as why the hell shouldn't she have?

But when the waiter brought our dinner up that night she suddenly blew the lid off of things. One minute he was chuckling and just being pleasant as waiters will; and the next minute he was out the door so fast his jacket tails were flying. I don't exactly remember what it was Elizabeth said to him. But I knew it was the wrong thing. And before I knew what was happening she was telephoning the manager and reporting this boy for insulting us.

"For Christ's sake," I said, when I finally got my breath, "what did you do that for, Elizabeth?"

"I'm sorry, Joe," she said. "I should have let you do it."

"Do what? Why should I have done anything?"

"Oh?" Her mouth tightened, then relaxed. "I know you've been thinking about business matters, dear. But if you'd noticed—"

"I tell you what I have noticed," I said. "I've noticed you standing right out in the middle of Stoneville, gabbing and laughing with some washwoman and her ragged-assed pickaninnies until—"

"Don't use words like that, Joe!"

"All right, then, they were just ragged, but—"

Well, how can you argue with a person like that? Someone that's absolutely determined to miss the entire point of a conversation?

I said, "Well, hell, let's forget it and go to bed." And we went, and there wasn't any more argument the rest of that night. But I still felt bad about getting this boy in trouble and maybe letting ourselves in for a lot of rotten service. And, like she always knew, Elizabeth knew that I was bothered.

When we went down to breakfast the next morning, the waiter captain gave us a funny look and led us over to a table in the middle of the dining-room. And then he snapped his fingers, and this same boy we'd had the night before came running over.

"George wants to apologize for his conduct," the captain said. "I'm sure you'll have no more trouble with him."

"Sure, why not," I said. "Just give us a menu and skip it. We'll get along all right."

I almost jerked the menus out of the waiter's hands, and shoved one at Elizabeth; and I got behind the other one fast. But it wasn't any go. Elizabeth wasn't ready to drop it until I looked like a complete damned fool.

"Why, sure, everything's okay," she said, letting out with a big laugh. "George and I are pals, aren't we, George?" And right in front of everyone she reached out and grabbed his hand and shook it.

We ate breakfast. I guess.

We got out of there and went for a long, fast walk. Elizabeth didn't say anything and neither did I. It wasn't until noon, after we'd eaten at a little hamburger joint in the town, that we got to speaking to each other again. And then it wasn't so good.

I did all I could, God knows. I admitted she'd played me for a chump, and tried to laugh it off. But right in the middle of my trying to make a joke of it she busted out bawling, and then she ran back to the hotel by herself.

I guess this waiter George must have been a pretty good boy because I had to pay the captain fifty bucks to fire him. That made things a little more comfortable; and after a day or two—a night or two, I should say—Elizabeth and I were beginning to feel that marriage wasn't such a bad deal after all.

We were a little edgy with each other, but, generally, I'd say that that feeling lasted on through our honeymoon and for several months afterward. It wasn't until I put Bower out of business that we had another real blowup.

"But you just couldn't have done it, Joe!" she said. "The Bowers are one of the oldest families in town, and they've always been good friends of ours. You can't deliberately ruin people like that."

"I'm not ruining them," I said. "If Bower wants to start another show it's all right with me."

"You know he can't start another one!"

"Well, that's his fault, then," I said. "I've got to protect our investment. It's up to him to look after his. What could be fairer than that?"

She sat and stared at me for a long time, and I began to get nervous. There wasn't any reason why I should have, but I couldn't help myself.

"Well, what's wrong?" I said.

"What do you think, Joe?"

"I don't think anything," I said. "All I know is that I work my can off trying to put us on a good spot and you can't do anything but find fault with me. Whose side are you on, anyhow? Mine or Bower's?"

"Do I have to take sides against people who've never done me any harm?"

"Look," I said. "This is business, Elizabeth. You just can't—"

"Never mind, Joe. I think I understand."

The smile she gave me wouldn't have fooled me later on, but it did at the time. And when she said of course she was on my side, where else would a wife be? I was completely taken in.

I went ahead and told her about the other things I had planned. How I could get the work done on a new house for nothing. How I could get the marquee and other stuff for next to nothing. How I could use them to get credit to pay the bills that couldn't be ducked. How we could run the house union at less expense than it cost to scab.

I must have shot off my mouth for an hour. And then, since everything seemed to be going so well, and we hadn't been married very long—

We went up to the bedroom, and that—it—was the craziest goddam thing that ever happened to me. Action? Sure; as much as you'd get on a roller coaster. Affection? The only twenty-dollar girl I ever had gave me a lot less. Heat? Like a furnace. It was lovely and wonderful, and so goddam phony I felt myself gagging right into her mouth.

I jumped up and began jerking on my clothes.

"All right," I yelled, "have it your way! I'll let everything slide, and you can have your goddam rattrap back as it stands and I'll clear out!"

"But I don't want you to clear out, Joe." She got up and stood in front of me. "I happen to love you."

"Damned if you don't," I said. "Just leave me alone. I won't bother you again."

"And I want you to bother me, too. Perhaps I'm a little disappointed in—in things, but—"

"You're disappointed?" I said. "What the hell do you think I am?"

She didn't answer that one, and I went ahead flinging on my clothes, trying not to look at her.

I finished dressing and started for the door, and she got in front of me.

"Well?" I said.

"Is this better, Joe?" she said. Then, *cr-aack!* She slapped me. "Do you like that better?"

And before I could come to my senses, before I could get over someone who was supposed to be a lady acting like a four-bit floozy, she'd shoved me out the door and locked it.

Well, I built the show. I did the other things I've told you about. And every once in a while, during those first few years, I thought we were going to be able to straighten things out and get along like married people should.

I thought so the strongest when she got pregnant, but then she miscarried and it was worse than ever. It was like I mentioned a while back. I never knew what she was going to do. I was never sure whether her actions and words meant one thing or whether they meant another.

About all I could ever be sure of was that she hated my guts, and that she hated them most right when she claimed to be loving me the loudest.

The funny part about it all was that with all her high-toned sneering, she wasn't too good to profit by the corners I cut. She insisted on keeping the show in her name, and she made almost as big a job of running it as I did. Not that anything she ever did was a damned bit of help, but she kept her hand in and held in there right on up to the end.

No, I don't think she was ever afraid of my skipping out if I wasn't tied down. And I don't think the main idea was to humiliate me, although that may have been part of it. I think—no, I don't, either. If I really thought that, then nothing would make sense.

I don't think I mentioned that she fired Carol that afternoon she caught her in my room. Well, she did, and I let her. It didn't look like I had much grounds for argument, and I figured I'd see Carol later and slip her some money and fix it up.

Carol packed up her things, or started to. Before she could finish Elizabeth called her down to the living-room.

"I'm partly to blame for this," she said to us. "Perhaps, by bringing Carol into this house, I'm entirely to blame. At any rate, I'm ready to assume some of the responsibility for it. Carol, exactly what are your feelings toward Mr. Wilmot?"

"None of your business," said Carol.

"And yours toward Carol, Joe?"

"There's no use in me saying anything," I said. "You've already got your mind made up."

"I see. Well, in preference to having this affair carried on around the countryside, I think Carol had best stay here. Go and unpack your things, Carol."

Carol looked at me, and I nodded. After she'd left the room Elizabeth stood up.

"I'm going to give you a little time to decide exactly what you want to do, Joe. And when you do reach a decision I expect you to stick by it. Do you understand?"

"Maybe I've already decided," I said.

"And?"

"Let's say I'm about as sick of you as you are of me."

"All right," she said. "Now, the little matter remains of what to do about it."

From where I sit now I'd say she thought she had me; that she knew there wasn't anything I could do and that I'd have to backwater on the deal. Looking back I'd say that she wasn't really thinking about the insurance when she agreed to settle for twenty-five grand. It was just her way of saying that she wouldn't trade at all.

I don't mean that she wanted me herself, because everything that she'd ever done or said pointed to the fact that she didn't. But she wasn't going to let Carol have me, either. Not Carol. She didn't hate Carol, exactly; she didn't think enough of her even to do that. It was Carol who did the hating and she did a good job of it. But—

But that's beside the point.

The insurance did get mentioned, and there was just one way we could cash in on it. And when I laid the plan out, little by little, Elizabeth went for it. It surprised me, but she did. She even took full charge of the plans pushing them along faster than I would have myself.

Carol thought it was all a gag, that Elizabeth was just trying to land her and me in trouble. But I didn't and don't think so. Elizabeth didn't need to pretend anything. She was in the saddle. And there was no way she could have made trouble for us without involving herself.

Why did she try to burn herself up there toward the last? The answer to that is, she didn't. It just looked that way. She knew every trick to that rewind motor. She knew just how much she could play around with that short-circuited cord without being in danger. I didn't move as fast as she thought I would and consequently she almost had herself a funeral party. But, anyway, it was a good trick and it almost worked.

If it hadn't been for Carol, for what had happened between us—And, yes, I guess Carol had been doing a little thinking, too, which was why things turned out as they did.

Carol could so some pretty straight thinking even if she didn't always come up with the straight answers. Word for word, I can still remember what she said that first night we talked about the murder.

"Why do you want to do it?" she said, staring hard at Elizabeth. "That's the part I don't get."

Elizabeth shrugged. "It seems that some move is indicated."

"By Joe and me, maybe. You don't need to stick your neck out."

"Well—shall we say I'm trying to be co-operative?"

"Don't make me laugh!"

"I wish I could," Elizabeth said. "Almost anything would be an improvement over your normal expression. However! I need a minimum of twenty-five thousand dollars to leave, and—"

"You've got a lot more than twenty-five thousand without leaving."

Elizabeth sighed and shrugged, as much as to say Carol was making a damned fool of herself. "There's not much more for me to say, is there? Think whatever you like."

"I am," said Carol, real slow. "And I—I don't understand—"

19

I felt sick driving home from the city after leaving Al,
kind of like I was catching the flu. The outside of my
body was warm enough, maybe a little too warm, but
inside I was cold. Shivering.

But sick or just scared sick, however you want to
put it, I couldn't help but admire the way Sol Panzer
had laid his plans. They added up to a knot behind my
ear, but I still had to admire them. By God, they were
perfect.

Or do you get it?

A stunt like Sol was pulling takes a lot of preparation
and a lot of dough. He had to have his stocks rigged for
the jump; he had to be able to show that he wasn't
bluffing. Just an announcement to the newspapers of
what he intended doing wouldn't be enough. The
papers wouldn't go for it and neither would the
suckers. The architect's plans would have to be
drawn and the construction contracts signed, and
money earmarked for the building. And, of course, the
film exchanges would have to be lined up.

Up to that point, there was almost no chance of a
leak, of someone's taking the edge off his surprise. Sol
was dealing with people he controlled. He could make
it worth their while to stay mum, and make 'em wish

they'd never been born if they didn't. The outsiders might *think* he was up to something, but they wouldn't know what it was. Their one chance of finding out would be when he bought a location. So?

So, he hadn't bought any. He hadn't risked having an option or a lease or a sale traced back to him. He didn't need to. I had the location he wanted, and when he got ready he'd step in and take it off my hands. I'd have about ten minutes to make up my mind. I could take a few grand and get out, or take nothing or next to it later on. I might cause him a little trouble, but it wouldn't make me anything. I'd take what he offered, whatever it was. I'd have to.

If I was still around . . .

I got into Stoneville a little after dark and drove around the square a few times, trying to make up my mind what to do. I was afraid to go home; I didn't know what I was going to say to Carol. I was afraid to go to the show; I didn't know what I could say to Hap. Finally, I parked across from the house, in front of Bower's old place, to give myself a little time to think; and I hadn't much more than shut my motor off before Andy Taylor was there, poking his head in the window.

"Been looking for you, Joe," he said. "Figured it was about time you an' me had a little talk."

"What about?" I said.

"I reckon you know."

"What do you think you've got on me, Andy?"

"I don't know, Joe. I ain't got the slightest idea. But I know I got somethin'."

"All right," I said. "I'll see you in a day or two. I'm sick and worn out right now. I think I'm coming down with the flu."

"Don't wait too long, Joe." He cackled. "I might talk to someone else."

He showed signs of needling me some more, so I mumbled something about business and walked across the street to the show.

Mrs. Artie Fletcher was in the box office, filing and buffing her fingernails and looking like she'd stab anyone that bothered her. You know, efficient and attractive like a cashier ought to look. Harry Clink-scales, my half-witted doorman, was doing his best, too, to run people off. He kept tossing grains of popcorn into the air and catching them in his mouth, stumbling around the lobby with his head thrown back and his mouth open about a foot. I wished to God a light bug would drop down it.

When he saw me he stopped and wiped his greasy hands on his uniform. My uniform.

"That's a good act, Harry," I said. "What'll you take to put it on inside?"

He grinned like an ape. "There was a guy here to see you a little while ago, Mr. Wilmot."

"A gentleman, Harry?"

"Yessir."

"What was his name?"

"Dunno. He didn't tell me."

"Well, that was pretty dumb of him, wasn't it?" I said. "What did he say when you asked him?"

Harry got kind of red in the face. "I think I know who he was, Mr. Wilmot. I think it was that guy— that gentleman from the insurance company."

"Oh," I said.

"He said he'd stop back later on in the evening."

"Good," I said; and I went on in and up to the projection booth.

Hap had just put on a new reel and was leaning back

against the rewind table, watching the picture through the port. The booth speaker was roaring; the sound was too loud. It gets that way early in the evening when there aren't enough people in the house to provide the right kind of acoustics.

Hap turned down the control a little, and wiped the sweat from his face and arms with a dirty towel.

"This is a veritable blast furnace, laddie. Why is it you didn't air-condition the booth when you did the rest of the house?"

"Why should I?" I said. "I don't sell any seats up here."

"Uh-*hah*," he said, narrowing his eyes at me. "Right to the mark, as usual, eh? Well, what luck in the city?"

"Nothing," I said. "None. I didn't get to see Panzer."

"Ah? You had your eyes closed?"

"No. He was out of town."

He took a step toward me, and I moved out of the way. He pulled a reel out of the film cabinet, slipped it into the off-projector, and flipped the switch on the arc.

"You're a bloody liar, old man. You're a blasted, stinking, filthy liar."

"For Christ's sake, Hap," I said. "Give me a little time! This thing hit me out of a clear sky. What the hell, anyway? I've got the insurance money coming."

"Have you, now? I wonder."

"I will if you—if—"

"Maybe it won't be left to me."

"How do you mean?"

"Your now-vacationing projectionist and I have been having some nice long talks. Got quite pally, young Nedry and I have."

"If you don't stop trying to pump him," I said, "he

will suspect something. Leave him alone, Hap. He doesn't know anything."

"I wish I were confident of that. He's dropped several sinister hints. He's intimated that he isn't going to be around very long, that he's got certain information which, transmitted to Blair—who's been after your scalp a long time, I understand—will get him a transfer to one of the city houses."

I laughed. I'd been wondering why Jimmie and Blair were running around together.

"Blair's letting his wishbone get in the way of his brain," I said, "and Jimmie is just hungry enough to string him along. He'll be right here as long as I want him."

"Oh? Are you—"

"I don't blame Jimmie for trying. Those city locals only have their charters open about an hour out of the year, and only the insiders know when that is. If some floater does get the word, all they have to do is give him an examination no one could pass or put the initiation fee out of his reach."

"I know all that, laddie."

"Well, Blair isn't going to go to all the expense and trouble of fixing things up unless Jimmie gives him some real dirt, and Jimmie can't because he doesn't have any. He's demanding the transfer before he talks."

"I don't know. It looks like Jimmie would have to know something. Suppose Blair gives him the transfer? What's his story going to be?"

"He won't need any. He can tell Blair to go laugh up a rope. He'd be in then, and out of Blair's jurisdiction."

"Well, I hope you're right, laddie. I sincerely hope so. For my sake."

"I'm right," I said. "By the way, don't you want me to give you a relief?"

"Oh, no. Nedry'll be along in a few minutes. He gives me a relief twice a day."

"Oh," I said. "Well, that's pretty nice of him."

"Isn't it, though?"

"Well, good night," I said.

"Cheerio! And remember—on your toes. I'm not waiting around here forever."

He started the off-projector, slid the port on the other one, and began unthreading the run-reel of film. I took a good long look at the back of his head and went downstairs again.

It wasn't much different from three thousand other nights. People strolling by, walking up to the box office or stopping to look at the lobby cards, asking how I was and being asked how they were. Now and then a car would pass by slow, and there'd be a light tap on the horn; and I'd turn around and wave and be waved at. A couple of bobby soxers stood up near the popcorn machine, giggling and talking to Harry, and watching me out of the corner of their eyes. Overhead, up above the marquee, the thirty-foot sign went on and off, spelled and flashed, painting the street and the cars green and red. Without looking, without even noticing, I knew when it went

B-A-R-C-L-A-Y, then BARCLAY, then *BARCLAY*.

I remembered all the arguments Elizabeth and I had had about that sign. How I'd hated it at first, yeah, how I'd hated her, not because I wanted my own name up there but because she didn't; because she wasn't as proud of Wilmot as she was of Barclay. And what did it matter? What did it really matter, anyway? Everyone knew who'd built the house. People always know those things. And Elizabeth was the last of the Barclays, and it was the oldest family in the county.

When people haven't got anything but a name you

can't blame them for leaning on it. And maybe—just maybe—that wasn't her reason. Maybe it was her way, as she'd put it, of being responsible. Of backing me up before the whole damned world.

Oh, hell . . .

I'd got hot up in the booth, and now I was beginning to chill. I passed a word or two with Mrs. Fletcher, and crossed the street to my car.

I got in and rolled up the windows, and lighted a cigarette. I let my head lie back against the seat and tried to rest. Maybe I dozed a little, but I don't think so. I think I was just so wrapped up in worrying about Carol and Elizabeth and Hap Chance and Andy and Sol Panzer and wondering what I was going to do that I was deaf and blind to everyone else.

I don't know how long Appleton stood outside the car looking in at me. But finally I rolled my head and there he was.

I kind of jumped, and then I opened the door and let him in.

20

"Gloating over the scene of your victory?" he said.

I didn't get what he meant.

"The show here," he said. "I understand you put your competitor out of business."

"Oh, yeah," I said. "No. I was just sitting here. Figuring on whether I wanted to eat a bite before I went home."

"By the way, I went to your show yesterday."

"I meant to give you some passes," I said. "I don't think I have any with me, but—"

"Forget it, Joe. It all goes on the expense account. But I wanted to ask you about those loges. Do you think they're safe?"

"I pay extra coverage for them," I said.

"Well." He laughed. "That makes everything all right, then. As long as you're covered."

I knew I'd made a dumb remark and that he was digging me, but I didn't particularly give a damn. My nerves were on edge. I was too sick and worried to think.

"I took a look at your exits, too, Joe. You know our state fire laws require two rear exits in a picture show."

"I've got two," I said.

"You've got a double door closing on the same jamb."

"It's good enough for the fire commissioner."

"Oh? Well, if it's good enough for him, who are we to quibble?"

He laughed again and nudged me, and I wanted to sock him. A guy can't be on his toes all the time.

"How are you getting along with your investigation?" I said. "About wound up?"

"Well—hardly," he said. "Those things take a lot of time, you know."

"I guess I don't know," I said. "The thing seems simple enough to me. The legal authorities are satisfied. I've been paying in premiums for ten years; and you've had plenty of time to find out if there was anything wrong. It looks to me like I'm entitled to a settlement or a damned good explanation."

He didn't get a bit sore. At least, he didn't show it.

"Well, that's the way it looks to you," he said. "Now I'll tell you how it looks to us. We don't have anything more to gain from you. You won't be carrying insurance on your wife, naturally, and the chances are that you'll drop your own. We don't want to pay you. We won't if we can get out of it."

"Thanks," I said. "I'm glad to know what kind of an outfit I'm dealing with."

"Don't quote me, Joe—don't mind my calling you Joe, do you? I'd hate to have to call you a liar."

"You may have a chance," I said. "I don't want anything I'm not entitled to, but—"

"Oh, sure you do. We all do. That's like saying you don't want anything more out of a thing than what you put into it. Where's the percentage in a deal like that? But you were threatening to sue us?"

"No, I wasn't threatening," I said. "I wouldn't want to sue unless—"

"And I don't think you will, Joe. You're too smart. There isn't a court in the land that wouldn't allow us from three months to a year to make our investigation. The chances are I'll have my report ready long before that. We haven't refused to pay the claim. We won't unless we have reason to."

I began to get hold of myself.

"Skip it," I said. "There's no hurry. I guess I was just sore because you knocked the house. I know those loges and exits aren't right, but I can't do everything at once. I haven't had a lot to work with."

"Sure. That's all right, Joe."

"But I'm kind of curious. Would you mind telling me something?"

"My life story if you want it."

"Maybe I'm stepping out of line and if I am, just say so. But—well, just what is there to investigate? I mean, it all looks pretty much cut and dried to me. The fire wiped out everything and—"

"Not everything, Joe."

"Well. You know what I mean."

"But you don't know what I mean. The most important clue to any disaster is the man who profits by it. Don't take that the wrong way. I'm not implying anything."

"How do you work on a clue like me?"

"Well, I don't slip around, dropping sly hints and giving people the wink. Nothing so crude as that, Joe. It's more a matter of moving around, observing and listening, gathering impressions, figuring out whether you're the kind of guy that would—"

"I suppose you try to put yourself in the—the other fellow's place, too."

"No. No, I don't, Joe." Rolling down the window, he threw out the butt of his cigarette and lighted another one. "In the first place that requires a preconceived notion of what the other fellow is; I'm making up my mind about him before I ever go to work on him. What kind of an investigation is that?"

"I've never thought about it that way," I said. "You hear the expression used so often, putting yourself in the other fellow's place—"

"It's bad business all the way around, Joe. If you put yourself in the other man's place often enough you're very likely to get stuck there. Some of your worst criminals began their careers as officers of the law. There's probably a higher incidence of insanity among psychiatrists than any other group. I remember a case I worked on several years ago—"

He paused and gave me a glance as much as to ask if he was boring me. I told him to go on. He was an easy guy to listen to, and I didn't want to go home.

"It was a murder, Joe. Just about the messiest job I've ever seen. A woman was literally clawed, clawed and chewed to death. Obviously, the murderer was a degenerate or a lunatic; we needed an expert on morbid psychology to get to the bottom of the crime. One of the best men in the country lived right there in the neighborhood, so, with the permission of the authorities, we called him in.

"Well, the police threw out the well-known dragnet, pulled in all the twist-brains they could lay hands on, and this guy went to work. And, Joe, by God, it was enough to make your flesh crawl to watch him. He'd sit there in a cell with some bird that you and I wouldn't touch with a ten-foot pole—the sort of bird that does things a lot of newspapers won't print—and he'd pal right up to him. He'd talk to him like a long lost brother. He'd find out what special sort of craziness this guy went in for, and for the time being he'd be the same way. If you closed your eyes and listened, you wouldn't know which one was doing the talking. And, yet, he was one of the most likable guys I've ever known. He talked my language, too. We seemed to click.

"We got to where we saw quite a bit of each other outside the line of business. He'd drop in on me a night or two a week, or I'd run in on him. We'd have a few drinks and a bite to eat, and bat the breeze around. And, gradually, without knowing I was doing it, I began to get his guard down. He started tipping his hand."

Appleton shook his head, started fumbling for another cigarette. I gave him one, and held a match.

"For God's sake," I said. "Let's hear the rest of it."

"He had a big German shepherd, Joe; a big brute that was a hell of a lot more wolf than it was dog. And I began to notice—he and that dog were a lot alike. Sometimes he'd snap at a sandwich or a piece of food just like the dog. Sometimes there'd be a trace of growl in his voice, or he'd scratch the back of his head with that stiff, rapid stroke a dog uses. Sometimes they even looked alike.

"The payoff came one night when he started to play with the dog. It started off as a romp, but before it was over they were down on the floor together, snapping and slashing and clawing, yeah, and barking. Both of 'em. And when I got the cops in they turned on us— the two dogs. Wolves. I don't need to tell you who our murderer was."

I shivered. He gave a short laugh.

"Not nice, huh, Joe?"

"I think I'm coming down with a cold," I said. "I've been having chills all evening."

"Well, I'll shove off and let you go. How about dinner some night this week?"

"Sure," I said. "But don't rush off. Tell me some more about this guy."

"What about him?"

"Well, why did he choose to be a dog? It doesn't seem to make sense. I can understand how a guy who worked with crooks all the time might turn out to be a crook, but—"

"He was a man of innate and extraordinarily fine sensibilities, Joe. And a man has to identify himself with something. He has to be able to picture himself as being some certain thing. If he can't, he's helpless. There's no motivation, no guide for his acting and thinking."

"Yeah," I said. "That's right, isn't it?"

"This man couldn't identify himself with the human race. He appeared to be able to do it with extreme ease, but actually he was losing a little of his character and personality with every contact. In the end, there wasn't anything left; nothing but the idea that humanity was pretty rotten. So—"

"I see," I said.

I shivered again, and he reached for the door.

"You ought to be in bed, Joe. I've got to be going, anyway. I've got another case to handle. Going to be on the jump for the next few days."

"Where's the fire this time?"

He shook his head. "It's not in my line, but as long as I'm here I'm taking a crack at it. It's a disappearance case. Some dame is supposed to have come out here from the city a few days ago, and she hasn't been heard of since."

"The hell!" I said. "What do you know about that?"

And he gave me a funny look.

"You don't need to be polite, Joe; I'm not interested in it, either. We get a hundred like it every year."

"But—but where could she disappear to in a town this size?"

"She couldn't; I'll turn her up in a few days. She's a houseworker; came out here to take a job. That narrows it down a lot. There aren't many people here who hire household help."

"No," I said. "Uh—how did you know she disappeared, anyway? Who reported it?"

"Her former landlady. She didn't have any relatives, it seems, and she owed this landlady a hell of a big bill. So, as a gesture of good faith, she switched a little paid-up policy she had—actually it would just about take care of her burial expenses when she died—to her landlady. That is, she named her as beneficiary until such time as she could clear up her debt. Well, she left the city in a hurry and was supposed to send for her baggage, and she hasn't done it. Naturally, the landlady is sure—she hopes—that something has happened to her, and she comes down on us."

"Y-Y-You're pretty sure y-you can f-f-find—"

"How can I help it? Say, you have got a chill, haven't you?"

My teeth were clattering too hard to answer. I nodded, and he said good night and got out. Up on the curb he hollered at me not to forget our dinner date; and I nodded again.

I backed the car out into the street, made a U-turn, and headed for home. As I started to angle around the square, I glanced into the rearview mirror. He was still standing where I had left him. Up on the curb, with his hat thrust back and his hands on his hips.

Watching me.

21

I must have been off my nut by the time I got home. I had to be to do what I did. I ran up the steps almost before the car had stopped rolling. I pushed the door open, half fell inside, and stood leaning against it.

"Elizabeth," I panted. "Elizabeth—"

And, of course, it wasn't Elizabeth. But even when I realized that, I couldn't come to my senses. It only made me worse.

I started to say that I was sorry, that Elizabeth's name had just slipped out; but I felt so ugly and scared, I guess, that it acted on her. And when it did she wasn't something I cared about hurting. She got me in the same way Elizabeth had used to.

It was all I could do to keep from slugging her.

"You—you muddle-headed bitch. Goddam—damn you! Didn't know where she was going, huh? Everything was all right, huh? Now they got us they got us *they got us!* They—"

I don't know what I said, the words were coming so fast and so mixed up, but somehow Carol got the sense of it.

"She didn't, Joe! She didn't know. I swear that she didn't!"

"Huh? How—"

"She was too anxious for the job to ask questions, and I slid over it. I told her I was hiring her for a friend. I told her I'd give her the exact address after we got here. I slid over it that way. She didn't know a thing until we got on the bus!"

"She called from somewhere! Or maybe she wrote! Her landlady—"

"I tell you, she didn't, Joe! She *did not!* I was with her every minute."

"But Appleton—"

"Don't you see, Joe? It's someone else. It's another woman. It *must* be."

"Oh," I said. "Oh—"

My knees were about to give way under me. I wobbled over to the lounge and sat down.

"You're sure about everything, Carol? Elizabeth got away all right?"

"Yes."

"And the woman? No one saw you, heard you, when—"

"No," said Carol. "We were all alone. We—she knew what was coming, right at the last, but there wasn't anything she could do. No one would hear her. I was stronger than she was. She didn't even try to fight. She—"

"Carol," I said. "For God's sake. You don't need to draw me a picture."

"I was just trying to tell you, Joe. Everything's all right. There's nothing to be afraid of."

The funny, intent look went out of her eyes. She turned them in toward the bridge of her nose and pursed out her lower lip. And then she blew upward at the little wisp of hair that had fallen over her forehead.

That got me, just like it always had. All at once we

were right back where we'd been that Sunday afternoon when she'd come into my room in her made-over clothes, and I'd felt so damned sorry for her I didn't know whether to laugh or cry.

"Come here, Carol," I said; and she came there, over to the lounge.

I gave her a grin and squeezed her hand, and after a minute she slid close to me.

"I'm sorry," I said. "That Appleton guy got me rattled. You know how you'd feel if you had a piece of news like that thrown at you."

"Yes," she said. "I'd know."

"I meant to tell you I was going into the city but I didn't have a chance. I had to leave in a hurry."

"Did you?"

"Yes, I did."

"Why?"

"Business. I could tell you, but you wouldn't understand."

"Oh."

"All right, 'oh,' then," I said. "It's the truth. God, Carol, I'm out in front in this deal! I can't stop and explain every time I turn around. I've got to do what I think's best."

"I know."

"Well, then?"

She hesitated, then turned and looked squarely at me. Or as squarely as she could with those eyes of hers.

"Will you answer me one question, Joe?"

"Certainly, I will."

"And tell the truth? Wait a minute, Joe! I didn't mean to insult you. But I've just got to know."

"All right, shoot," I said.

"Is there something wrong at the show?"

I shook my head. I couldn't find my voice right then.

"You're not—that's the truth, Joe?"

"Of course, it's the truth. What are you driving at? What could be wrong?"

"I don't know," she said. "But there *is* something wrong. There's something wrong somewhere, and you're afraid to tell me about it. That's what—w- what I c-can't stand. Your being afraid of me."

"Aw, hell," I said, trying to put my arm around her. "Why would I be afraid of you?"

"It's no good asking each other questions, Joe." She brushed at her eyes. "What we need is answers. We're in this together, but we're pulling different ways. You don't trust me."

"It don't—doesn't—look like you trusted me a hell of a lot, either."

"I love you, Joe. Sometimes you love a person so much you can't trust them. It's for their own good that you don't."

"Well," I said. "I don't know what you want me to say."

"I—I guess there isn't much to say."

I jumped to my feet and headed for the kitchen. And I didn't stop or look around when she called me. Things had been coming at me too fast; I didn't have anything left to fight with. I had to do something quick or I knew I'd be yelling the truth at her. *You're goddam right I'm afraid! You'd think I pulled you into this to get Elizabeth and me out of a hole! You think I'd sell anyone out! You—*

I got the cupboard door open and reached down the whisky bottle. I raised it, turning around, and she was standing in the doorway watching me.

The whisky never reached my mouth. I couldn't get it that high. It trickled out on my shirt front, and then the bottle dropped from my hand to the floor. And I followed it.

Instantly she was at my side, lifting me. And sick and dizzy as I was, the one thought that filled my mind was how much strength she had. I weigh around two hundred, but she hoisted me up and got me over to the table as easily as if I'd been a child.

"Joe, darling—What do you want me to do, Joe?"

"I'm sick." I kept repeating it. "I'm sick, Carol."

"Do you want me to get a doctor?"

"No!" No, I didn't want a doctor. He might give me something to knock me out, and I'd start raving.

"I'm just awfully tired and weak," I said. "Running around too much. Not eating. Got a chill—"

She put a hand to my forehead. "You've got a fever, too."

"I'd better go to bed," I said. "I get in bed and I'll be all right."

"All right, Joe."

She started to lift me again, but I held back. "We can't go on staying here alone, Carol. We'll have to have someone come in."

"Do you want me to call Mr. Chance?"

"Jesus, no! I mean I may be in bed several days. We want someone who can be around all the time. Get Mrs. Reverend Whitcomb. Take the car and go after her. She'll do anything to get a few square meals."

She got up slowly, kind of hanging back. "Couldn't I just call her, Joe?"

"How would she get over here? The Whitcombs don't have a car. Now, go on and go after her before it gets any later."

"But—but I don't drive very well. I don't like to drive after dark."

"You drive good enough. You drove all the way home from Wheat City after dark, didn't you?"

"All right," she said. "I'll go right away."

After she'd gone, I went on sitting at the table for a few minutes, thinking or trying to; something tickling my mind. Something important. But the idea wouldn't come. I was too tired.

I don't know what time it was when she and Mrs. Whitcomb got back. I was already in bed and asleep.

Back in reform school, once, some big-shot lawyer talked to us at chapel, and he made the statement that nature hated a crime. "Nature abhors a crime," was the way he put it.

At the time, it struck me as being just some more of the grapefruit they were always squeezing out to us. It seemed to me that for a guy that had nature against him, he was doing pretty well. But now, twenty-five years later almost, I was beginning to see what he meant.

We'd planned everything perfectly. By all the laws of logic nothing could go wrong. And, yet—well, why say it?

On top of everything else I was afraid I was losing my nut.

I woke up early the next morning and tiptoed into the bathroom. I got a drink of water at the sink, and stood staring out the window. And there was the garage, just as big as day. Yeah, it was there. The old barn with the cupola that had been made over into a garage. I saw it just as I had seen it for ten years. I don't know. Maybe the eye holds images that don't go away, that don't ever really go away. Maybe the average guy is so stuck on himself that everything he sees becomes important, and he won't give it up, not to himself, until he's past seeing and past remembering.

I don't know.

All I know is that I almost let out a yell that they could have heard over in the next county.

I had to put my hand over my mouth to hold it back.

I got back into bed, shivering, and finally dozed off again. But it wasn't good sleep. Not sound, I mean. I kept dreaming that Elizabeth was in the room with me. And it was like I was looking back or ahead on something that had happened.

She was climbing up on a chair to get something down from the ceiling—I don't know the hell what—and anyone could see that the chair was made out of straw and wasn't going to hold her up. But she kept climbing up on it and I'd run and catch her, and then she'd throw herself back in my arms and kiss me.

Then, there was a little guy that kept coming to the door and trying to get in. And there wasn't a damned bit of sense in her being afraid of him, because he was so damned little and funny-looking. But anyway he kept coming and I'd go to the door and tell him to get the hell out, and he'd beat it for a minute or two. And then I'd go back over to the bed and pull the covers off of Elizabeth, but instead of doing what I should have done I'd stand there and laugh. Because, dammit, I know it's crazy, but she'd turned into a statue. She had and she hadn't. We had to do it first or she would be, but if we didn't she was. And—

And then it was our wedding anniversary, it seemed like, and she was reminding me how, wherever we were, we'd promised that we'd always get together on our anniversary. And even dreaming, I knew it really was our anniversary, and I kind of remembered that we'd said that, that we'd promised like, I suppose, every couple does when they're first married.

She kneeled down at my side and put her hand on my forehead. She leaned forward and kissed me on the mouth.

And I woke up, and it was Carol.

"How are you feeling?" she whispered.

I blinked my eyes.

"All right," I said.

"Your fever seems to have broken."

"Yeah," I said, "I'm all right. Just weak."

"What would you like for breakfast?"

I told her just a little toast and coffee would do. "Better bring up some whisky, too. I'm chilling."

She was back in ten minutes or so with a tray. I sat up and made out like I was going to eat.

"You'd better run along, Carol. It won't look good for you to spend too much time up here."

"I—there's something I want to say to you, Joe."

"Well?"

"But I've got to know something first. I've got to know the truth. Do—do you really love me?"

"Oh, Jesus Christ!" I slammed down my coffee cup. "If you've got anything to tell me, spit it out! If you haven't, leave me alone for a while. We're not supposed to be together and I'm sick, and I've got a thousand and one things to think about. I'm sorry, but—"

"That's all right, Joe. I'm going."

"I do love you, Carol," I said. "You know that."

But she was already gone.

I took a bite or two from the toast, and put the rest in a bureau drawer under some shirts. I drank the coffee down halfway, and filled up the cup with whisky. After a second cup of the stuff, I felt pretty fair. I could have got up as well as not. But I stayed where I was. I wasn't ready to face people yet. Andy Taylor and Appleton and Happy Chance. Maybe I'd never be, but I sure wasn't now.

Around noon of the third day, right after I'd got through taking a bath, I heard a car coming up the lane from the road. I looked out the window to see who it was, but it was already up and in front of the house by then.

A minute or so later Carol tapped on the door, and I told her to come in.

"There's a man here to see you, Joe. He said to tell you it was Sol."

"Oh," I said. "Tell him to come up."

"Who is he, Joe? Is there—"

"Tell him to come up," I repeated.

She got that hard, stubborn look on her face like she used to get around Elizabeth. But finally she turned and went back downstairs, taking her time about it.

22

Sol Panzer looked more like a jockey than the owner of a ninety-house chain. He was maybe five feet tall, and he might have weighed a hundred and ten with his clothes wet. I guess he had something wrong with his vocal cords, because his voice matched up with the rest of him. It was thin and soft; not much more than a whisper.

If Carol tried to listen, and I figured she would, she wouldn't hear much.

He stood by the door a moment, looking at me out of the big horn-rimmed glasses he wore. Then he moved over to the bed like greased lightning, grabbed my hand and shook it, and dropped into a chair right in front of me.

"Joe," he said, speaking in his fast half-whisper. "I'm sorry to see you sick. I was sorry about Mrs. Wilmot. I hope you got our flowers. This is a nice place you have here."

"Thanks," I said. "Stick around and maybe you can buy it cheap."

"I'm sorry, Joe." He began to slow down. "It's nothing personal."

"That's all right. Have a drink."

"No, no. I never drink during business hours."

"If this is business," I said, "maybe we'd better get down to it."

"Cold turkey?"

"Without the stuffing."

"Well—a dollar and other valuable considerations."

"Remember me?" I said. "I own the place. How many valuable considerations?"

"Say, about five thousand."

I let out a grunt. "Five thousand wouldn't pay for my projectors and sound heads."

"Probably not, Joe."

"Then there's my chairs," I said. "Fifteen hundred of 'em with a factory list of eighteen seventy-five."

"You bought cheap. They'll run you twenty-two fifty, now."

"I've got a thousand yards of six-bucks-a-yard carpeting. I've got four grand in air conditioning. I've got—"

"Joe."

"Oh, all right," I said. "You don't want the stuff."

"I couldn't buy it if I did want it, Joe. I got friends in the theatrical supply line. Close friends, y'know. What would they think if I didn't patronize 'em? They'd be hurt, Joe. You know they would."

"Yeah," I said, "I guess they would."

I'd known how it was going to be. But I couldn't fight, and when a man can't fight the best thing he can do is stall.

"Well, Joe?"

"Well," I said. "Twenty-five grand isn't a bad price for the location. I'll take it."

"I don't speak very loud, Joe. Maybe you didn't hear me say five."

"Twenty."

"Five. But don't be afraid to beg, Joe. My way of refusing is very polite."

I took another drink and lighted a cigarette. I looked
down at the floor, pretending to study. Stalling.

"I don't know, Sol," I said. "Doesn't it strike you
that this is a pretty hard thing to do to a friend?"

"A friend, Joe?" He looked puzzled. "I hardly know
you when I see you."

"Make it an enemy, then," I said. "You're obligated
to come into this town. I don't know how much you're
already in on the deal, but it must be plenty. You've
got to come in, and I'm sitting on the spot you want."

"Yes, Joe?"

"Well, maybe you'd better take it from there."

He nodded and leaned back in his chair. "You got
bills outstanding, Joe. You got insurance to pay, you
got taxes to pay. You got a little bank loan, maybe two
of 'em. Not much. None of it amounts to much—*if*
you're running. But let your house go dark and see
how big all them little things are. See how fast people
start coming down on you. Then—"

"Oh, hell," I said. "I'm—"

"I'm not through, Joe. I could wait you out two-
three months, but I won't have to. I'm going to crack
down if you even look like you want to be stubborn.
I'm going to get you for that marquee you swindled me
on."

"You?" I said.

"Me. I was interested in that company. I still am. I
started watching you when you beat me on that deal. I
figured you were a man worth watching. I figured I
could make a lot more by letting the five grand ride
than cracking down on you. Funny, ain't it? If you'd
played square with me I never would have started
looking into Stoneville. I wouldn't have noticed the
kind of business you were building up."

"Hell, Sol," I said, "you shouldn't hold a grudge
over that. I didn't know it was your company."

His eyes closed for a second behind the big horn rims. "Joe," he said. Then he shook his head and sighed. "I don't hold any grudge, Joe. I'm just showing you what's going to happen if you try to hold me up. I'll sue you for that marquee; the actual price of it plus interest plus general losses due to having my product unjustly condemned. Do I make myself clear? I'm moving in. I'll either buy your lot or I'll take it."

"But five grand, Sol," I said. "That's no dough at all. You can do better than that. You know damned well you'll give the lot a book value of thirty or forty thousand."

"But it was my idea, Joe." He shrugged. "You can't expect to cash in on my ideas, can you?"

"What'll I do with my equipment? It's no good without a house to put it in."

"So I've heard. You gave your former competitor a hundred and fifty dollars for his stuff, didn't you?" He shrugged again, smiling out of the corner of his mouth. "Don't cry on me, Joe. On you tears don't look good. And don't stall me. That marquee deal ain't the only thing I've got on you. I can pile up stuff to the doors of the Barclay if I take a notion. You got the most remarkable record of chiseling I ever laid eyes on."

"I'm not trying to stall," I said. "I'm just trying to think. It seems like everything has come down on me at once. Being sick, and losing my wife, and now—"

"I know, Joe." His face softened a little. "But I'm not moving in tomorrow. You can run until the end of the season."

"You want an agreement to buy at the end of that time?"

"That's it."

"All right," I said. And I took the biggest, almost the biggest gamble I've ever taken in my life. "Give me your check for five thousand and we'll close the deal."

If he'd taken me up on it, I'd have been washed up. But I had a pretty good idea he wouldn't, and he didn't. You see? Why should he have made a special trip out from the city to bully me into selling something he could take?

"If you want it that way, Joe," he said slowly. "But for your own good I'd advise you to hold off. You've got to run until the end of the season. Selling now would ruin your credit."

"It wouldn't help it any," I agreed. "But I sup-posed—"

"I just wanted to reach an understanding with you. I'm not afraid of your trying to sell to someone else. No one's going to buy a big show property without a lot of investigation. I can muff any deal you try to make."

"I know," I said. "That's the deal, then. Five grand at the end of the season for the lot. I keep everything else."

"Providing you move it."

"That's understood."

He stood up and held out his hand. "We'll let the option slide, then, as long as we understand each other."

"You're the doctor, Sol," I said.

I walked him to the door, closed it, and poured myself another drink. I swallowed it just as I started to laugh, and for a minute or two I thought I was going to strangle. When Carol came in I was staggering around, sputtering and laughing like a hyena with the whooping cough.

She slapped me on the back and got a drink of water down me. Finally I began to get my breath back.

"You're drunk, Joe," she frowned. "You shouldn't get drunk at a time like this."

"Baby," I said. "I was never more sober in my life."

"Who was that man? What did he want?"

"That was Sol Panzer," I said. "Sol is the s-smartest—" I had to stop for a second, "showman in the business. He wanted to buy the Barclay."

"Oh?" She stiffened a little. "How much will he give you for it?"

"Nothing, baby. Nothing. And do you know why? Because he doesn't want it."

"But you just said—"

I didn't say anything for a minute. I just put my arms around her and squeezed until her breasts flattened against me, until the veins in them swelled and began to throb. Then I said, "Leave it to me, kid. Just a little longer. Leave it to me, and we'll pull out of this town with two hundred grand. Will you do that?"

I felt her nod, slow, unwilling. Eager.

"Yes, Joe. Yes!" she said. And: "Mrs. Whitcomb—she's taking a nap, Joe—"

Once, right at the last, like you will, you know, I looked into her face. Then, I closed my eyes and kept them closed.

23

Hap Chance called during the afternoon. I had Carol
tell him I was sleeping. Andy Taylor called, too; and I
had her tell him I'd see him that night. She called
Appleton for me and made a date for dinner. She was
curious, of course, but she didn't ask questions. I'd
taken care of that for a while, at least.

I drove down to the hotel about six. Appleton was
waiting for me in the lobby. We shook hands and
found a table in the dining-room.

"Well, Joe," he said, looking me up and down, "your
rest seems to have done you a lot of good."

"I needed one," I said. "I guess I've been going
around in a daze ever since the accident. I got to the
point where I couldn't go on any longer."

"That's the way it goes," he nodded, glancing at the
menu. "By the way, what's this talk about you having
a competitor in here?"

The glass of water I was holding almost slipped out
of my hands.

"Where did you hear anything like that?"

"Oh, it wasn't anything definite. Just a rumor."

"There's a rumor for every inch of film in show
business," I said. "Your statement was that there
was talk going around. I want to know where it's
coming from."

I could see that he didn't really know anything. There's always gossip in any good spot where one man has control. Someone will start talking about how much the showman must be making, and how there ought to be another show there. And, before you know it, the story gets twisted to where there *is* another house coming in.

"I've got a hundred-thousand-dollar investment here," I said. "If there's a rumor going around I want to know what there is to it, and who's spreading it."

"It wasn't anything, Joe. Just some wishful thinking, I guess. Let's forget it."

"I can't afford that kind of talk," I said.

For once he was on the defensive. "Let's forget it," he mumbled. "If I hear anything more, I'll put the damper on it."

He didn't have much to say during the meal. As soon as we had finished we went up to his room.

"Well, here we are, Joe," he said, grinning again. "The secret lair of Operator 31."

It was one of the sample rooms that salesmen use. Two of the big sample tables were fixed up for kind of a laboratory. He even had a little weight scale, and a centrifuge like they've got down to the creamery, only smaller. One of the tables was covered with stuff from the fire—little envelopes of ashes, pieces of wood, wire, and metal.

I looked away. There was a picture of a woman and a little boy on the dresser. The boy was about four, I imagine.

"Is that your boy?" I asked. "He looks a lot like you."

"That's him," he nodded. "Think he looks like me, huh? Not everyone can see the resemblance."

"Why, he's the spit and image," I said. "How old is he, about six?"

"Four. He wasn't quite four when that picture was taken."

"Well, he's certainly big for his age," I said. "I'd have taken him to be six, anyway."

Appleton nodded, his smile a mile wide. "Yes, sir, he's a real boy. You ought to see him out playing ball with me when I'm at home. He's the craziest kid about baseball I ever saw, and he can really play, too. I mean, Joe, he's got baseball sense. He—"

He kind of shook himself, and gave me a wink.

"Damn you, Joe!"

"What's the matter?"

"Let it go. What do you know that's new since I saw you last?"

"Nothing much. I don't know whether I told you last time that I'd talked with the county attorney. He's still confident that the fire was an accident."

Appleton wagged his head. "I'm inclined to agree with him, Joe. At any rate I'd probably say the same thing if I were a public servant."

"Now what do you mean by that?" I said.

"It's a public servant's job to serve the public, Joe. The living public."

"I guess that's a dirty crack," I said.

"Not at all. I'm not hinting that Mr. Clay is dishonest. He's in office. Mrs. Wilmot is dead. You're one of the city's most prominent citizens. Why should he go out of his way to prove something which, in all probability, didn't happen?"

"Well," I said, "I'm glad to hear you say that."

"You don't owe me a nickel, Joe."

"I got to thinking while I was sick," I said. "It seems like I must have made a chump of myself the first time I talked to you. Maybe the next time, too, but that time particularly."

"You're referring to what I said about the fire being incendiary?"

"That's it. I don't know why—"

"I'll tell you why. I didn't intend for it to register on you. I thought it was better for it to come over you gradually. Frankly, if you had gone around offering rewards for the murderer and evidence of your own innocence I'd have been exceedingly suspicious of you."

"Now, what am I supposed to say to that?" I said.

"Anything you like, Joe. The bars are down tonight. That's why I had you come up here."

"Okay. What do you think about things?"

"As I've said before, that it was an accident in all likelihood. Of course, you and Mrs. Wilmot didn't get along, but—"

"Who says we didn't?"

"You do. Everything about you says so. Everything I've learned about her says the same thing. But the fact that you were opposites doesn't mean that you would kill her. In fact, I'm confident that you loved her very much."

"Well, thanks," I said.

"It's none of my business, but would you mind telling me something? How did two people like you ever happen to get married?"

I laughed in spite of myself. It was such a hell of a crude thing to ask that instead of getting sore I felt sorry for him for doing it.

"I'll tell you why," I said, looking straight at him. "Every time she opened her mouth she put her foot in it. She was about to go on the rocks. I got sort of used to helping her out, and finally—well—"

"Mmm," he nodded. "That one, eh?"

"What do you mean?"

"Not a thing, Joe. Just thinking out loud. Mind if I ask another question?"

"Go right ahead."

"Well, this Farmer girl—Mrs. Wilmot strikes me as having been a well-educated, extremely fastidious person. How did she happen to take anyone like la Farmer into her home?"

It was something I'd always wondered about myself, and I didn't need to fake looking puzzled.

"There you got me," I said. "Elizabeth was pretty tight about money, and I thought at first that she might be trying to get a little cheap household help. But she wasn't tight that way, you know. She wouldn't have done something that went against her grain to save dough."

"I see."

"Anyway, we didn't need any help. There was just the two of us and I always ate out most of the time. On top of that, Elizabeth had her own way of doing things and nothing else would suit. It was more trouble showing Carol how to do things than it would have been to do 'em herself."

"Perhaps she just felt sorry for the gal."

"She didn't show it much. If I hadn't—well, if I hadn't prodded her now and then, Carol would have been pretty hard up for spending money and clothes and everything else."

"Oh? Weren't you a little out of practice at that sort of thing—charitable enterprise, I mean?"

"I don't think I like that," I said. "I'm in a tough business. I don't think I've been any tougher than I've had to be."

"Want to call it an evening, Joe?"

"Not unless you do. Go ahead. I can take it."

"Well, I was going to say, if this Farmer girl was a

baby doll the thing would be a lot more complicated—
or simple. A little thing like murder doesn't stop a
woman from getting a man she really wants—particularly if she thinks she's going to get to help him
spend a sum like twenty-five thousand. But Farmer
has nothing minus in my catalogue. I just can't
picture you making a play for her."

"Thanks," I said.

"So the girl is out, and you're out on that angle. Of
course, you get your wife's property in addition to the
twenty-five grand. But for all practical purposes you
already had the property, and you didn't need the
money. Not bad enough to kill for it. You have a good
income, a good business. You loved your wife. You
weren't chasing a dame. If it wasn't for certain events
in your early life—"

"So you've found out about that," I said. "That's a
hell of a thing to do! Drag up something a man did
when he was a kid, and smear him—"

He shook his head. "Keep your shirt on. We're not
smearing anyone, and we didn't drag it up. You did.
The company doesn't issue policies of this size without
some investigation."

"Hell," I said. "I was fourteen years old; I didn't
know my tail from straight up. I'd never been away
from the orphanage before. I didn't know what a seal
on a freight car meant. I just wanted to get out of the
snow. Tampering with interstate commerce! Hell, did
they think I was going to walk off with a sack of
cement? That's all there was in the car."

"It was a bum rap, all right."

"Bum rap?" I laughed. "You're telling me! Seven
years of sappings and kickings and doing work that
would break a man's back. Seven years, from fourteen
until I was twenty-one—'until I learned a proper

regard for the property of others'! It's things like that—that—"

I broke off, remembering.

"Go ahead and say it, Joe," said Appleton. "It's things like that that makes criminals."

"Okay," I said, "you're doing the talking."

"Do I look like a criminal?" He leaned back grinning, his hands clasped behind his head.

"What's that got to do with it?"

"I was in, too. Exactly the same number of years that you were."

"The hell!" I said.

"That's right. Borrowed a car for a joy ride, and the cops caught me. My old man wasn't very fond of me, anyhow, so I went right on over the road. No, things like that don't need to mean any more than we let 'em."

"But you said your company—"

"It's a fact they have to consider, certainly. It's tough, but that's the way it is." He sat brushing at his knee, looking down. "I'm sorry, Joe. I know pretty well how you feel. Can't you think of some logical explanation—some explanation that would be acceptable to the company—for the fire?"

"No, I can't."

"The motor was in good condition? There wasn't any possibility of a short?"

"Not a chance. If there had been any I'd have had it repaired."

"Sure. Naturally."

"It isn't the money so much," I said. "I'd just like to get things settled."

"Sure you would." He nodded sympathetically, studying me. "I'll tell you something, Joe, if you'll keep your mouth shut. I've been stringing you along a little. I've recommended payment on this case. I'm just waiting to mail my report."

"Waiting?"

"Orders." He smiled out of the corner of his mouth. "You're running in hard luck, Joe. You remember that missing dame I told you about?"

"Yes."

"Well, there's the rub. I've got to turn her up, and as long as I'm here and it isn't costing them anything extra the company's having me keep your case open. At least they think they are. As far as I'm concerned it's already closed. As soon as I find this woman I'll put a date on the report and shoot it in."

"Well," I said, "that's something." I wished I had been outside so that I could have taken a deep breath. Or let out a yell. Just of pure relief.

I didn't care if I never got the money. I was going to have plenty without it.

We talked until midnight about show business, and the war, and things in general. Finally I figured it was time for me to go.

We shook hands. "Got any leads on the woman yet?" I said.

"Oh, one or two, Joe. I'm expecting a break in the case any minute."

"Well, luck to you," I said.

"And to you, Joe. And, Joe—"

"Yeah?" I said. He'd opened the door and I was standing halfway out in the hall.

"Do yourself a favor. Do a little deep thinking about some of the stuff we've discussed here tonight. It may make you feel bad for a time, but you'll profit by it in the long run. It'll make it a hell of a lot easier for you to get along with yourself."

"You're not telling me much," I said.

"It's something you'll have to see, Joe. Good night, and take it easy."

"I'll do that," I said.

24

The front of the building was dark, but I could see a faint light in the back. I tapped on the window and rattled the doorknob. And in a couple of minutes Andy Taylor came shuffling around from behind the screen that separates his so-called office from his living-quarters.

I don't know whether he'd been in bed or not. He still had his clothes on, but I'd always had the idea he slept with them on most of the time.

"Kinda took your time about gettin' here, didn't you?" he said. "Come on in."

I followed him back to the rear of the building, and he put the coal-oil lamp he'd been carrying down on a packing-box. He didn't have any real furniture. Just a cot and some boxes and a little monkey stove. I sat down on the cot.

"So you decided to take me up," he said. "Well, well."

He moved a dirty pie plate and a coffee cup off of one of the boxes and sat down across from me. The light from the lamp made his beard seem redder than usual. He looked like the devil with a hat on.

"Not so fast," I said. "Take you up on what?"

"I don't know, Joe. I don't know."

"I got a burn on my hand," I said, "that's all. Anyone that works around electricity as much as I do is bound to get burned."

"Sure they are."

"Well?" I said.

"You were willing to cancel the lease on the Bower."

"I was willing to do that, anyway. I've been thinking for a long time that I hadn't treated you right on that lease."

"Yeah. I bet you did."

He rubbed his chin, looking straight into the flame from the lamp. For a minute I was afraid that I'd been too independent, that he wasn't going to walk into the trap.

Then he laughed, just with his mouth, and I knew everything was all right.

All he needed was a little steering.

"All right, Joe," he said. "I ain't got a thing on you. Not a thing. Why don't you just get up and walk out of here?"

"Okay," I said. "I will."

I got up slow, brushing at my clothes, and turned toward the door. He watched me, the grin on his wrinkled old face getting wider and wider.

"O' course," he said. "You know I'm going to tell Appleton about that burn."

"What for?" I said. "Why do you want to do that, Andy?"

"What do you care? As long as it don't mean nothing."

I shrugged and took a step toward the door. Then I let my face fall and I sank back down on the cot.

I heaved a sigh. "Okay, Andy. You win."

He nodded, his eyes puzzled. "Thought I would," he said. "Wonder why, though?"

I didn't say anything.

"That motor was in good condition. Elizabeth wouldn't have been foolin' around with it if it wasn't. Not Elizabeth."

"No," I said.

"And we know the fire wasn't set. There's proof positive of that."

"No," I said, "it wasn't set."

"And you were in the city when it happened."

"That's right. I was in the city."

"But there was something wrong, mighty wrong. So wrong that you're willin' to give me—how much are you willin' to give me, Joe?"

"What do you want?"

"Make me an offer."

"Well, I'm short of cash right now. But I could give you part of the money from the insurance."

"Not part, Joe. All."

"But, Jesus," I said. "All right, goddamit. All!"

He cackled and shook his head. "Huh-uh, Joe. I wouldn't touch that money. How would it look for me to plunk twenty-five thousand in the bank after a deal like this? Huh-uh! I just wanted to get some idea of what it was worth to you for me to keep quiet. Some basis for tradin'."

"Well, now you've got it."

"Yeah, now I've got it. And you know what I'm goin' to do with it, Joe? Somethin' I've been wanting to do for years."

"Spit it out," I said. "For God's sake, you know I've got to come across. What is it you want?"

"Nothing more than what you owe me, Joe. I had a good thing once, and you ruined it for me. Now I'm handin' you back the ruins and takin' your good thing."

I looked blank. "What the hell are you driving at?"

"I'm makin' you a swap, Joe. I'm going to give you the Bower for the Barclay."

You know, it was a funny thing. It was what I'd expected and wanted. It was what I'd been edging him toward from the start. But now that he'd fallen for it I didn't have to pretend to be sore or surprised.

It burned me up just as much as when I'd heard about Panzer moving in. It's funny; maybe I can't explain. But that show—that show—

No, I can't explain.

I came to my senses after a minute, but I kept on cursing and arguing awhile to make it look good.

"That's not reasonable, Andy," I said. "The Barclay's a first-class house. The Bower's just a rattrap."

"It wasn't always a rattrap. Maybe you can build it back up again."

"Like hell. I see myself building the Bower up with the Barclay as competition."

"Oh, I ain't no hog, Joe. I won't shut you out. Prob'ly wouldn't know how even if I wanted to."

"Why not do this, Andy," I said. "We'll be partners. I'll run the business, and we'll—"

He let out another cackle.

"Oh, no, we won't, Joe! I've had a little experience running things on shares with you. The first thing I knowed I'd be out in the cold."

"But how's it going to look," I said, "to make a trade like that? I ain't got any reputation for being crazy. People will know there's something screwy about the deal."

"Now, you're smarter'n that, Joe." He shook his head. "They won't know a thing more'n we tell 'em—

and I reckon neither you or I is going to talk. We'll make it a trade, plus other valuable considerations. Just like ninety-nine per cent of all real estate deals is made."

"But Appleton—"

"Appleton'll be gone from here when I take over. Like I said, Joe, I ain't operatin' no kind of business with you. You go ahead and operate the Barclay until the end of the season. I'll take it then."

"Andy, can't we—"

"Yes or no, Joe?"

"Oh, hell," I said. "Yes!"

He went up to the front and brought back some legal forms and his rickety old typewriter, and we finished the business then and there. We drew up a contract agreement to a transfer of deeds at the end of the season, and he gave me a check for a dollar and I gave him one, each carrying a notation as to what it was for.

That made the deal airtight, even without witnesses. There was no way either of us could back out.

I offered to shake hands as I was leaving, but he didn't seem to notice. I let it pass. He'd feel a lot less like shaking hands when the end of the season came.

It was about one in the morning, now. I debated going home and decided against it. It would save arguing and explaining, and, anyway, there wasn't much time for sleep. I wanted to be in the city when the business offices opened in the morning.

I went over to the show, got the clock out of the projection booth, and set the alarm for two hours away. I sat down in one of the loges, put the clock under the seat, and leaned back. The next thing I knew I was back as far as my memory went.

With my mother, or the woman I guess was my mother. I was living it all over again.

The big hand of the clock was pointing to twelve and the little one to six, and she was coming up the stairs, slow—slowly—like she always came; like she wasn't sure where the top was. Then a key scratched against the lock, and finally it turned, and the door opened. And she tottered over to the bed and lay down and began to snore.

She'd brought something in a sack with her, and she was half lying on it, and I had to squeeze and tug to get it. It was a piece of jelly roll and a hamburger, all squashed together, and I hogged it down. After that I felt through her pockets until I found the crisp green pieces of paper she always brought me; and I hid them in the bureau drawer with the others.

Then it was morning, and she was gone again. I filled my tin cup with cornflakes and canned milk, and ate it. And I played with the green pieces of paper and looked out the window; and I ate a little more of the cornflakes and milk.

The big hand of the clock pointed to twelve and the little one to six. It pointed to them, and passed them. I laughed about it, holding my hand over my mouth so no one would hear me.

I was still laughing when I went to sleep.

She was gone in the morning, but she was always gone in the morning. I ate some of the cornflakes and milk, and played with the green pieces of paper and looked out the window. And the big hand of the clock pointed to twelve and the little one to six, and—and—

It was like a dream inside of a dream. I was chewing the wrapper inside the cornflakes box, and the tip of my tongue was cut where I'd tried to stick it through the little hole in the milk can, and the water pitcher was red from my licking. I wasn't looking out the window any more. I was on the bed. I had been on the bed for a very long time, and the green pieces of paper were scattered all around me.

Then, and then, it was another room, and a big fat woman with crossed eyes, was holding me in her arms and rocking me.

"Mommy? Sure, now, an' we'll get you a whole raft of 'em! I'll be your mommy meself."

"My money! I got to have my money!"

"An' ain't I the one to know it, now? Bring his bundle in, Mike— That mess of whisky labels ..."

The alarm clock went off, and I woke up. I went into the men's lavatory and washed and headed for the city.

25

Sol Panzer didn't make nearly as much fuss as you might have thought he would. He was on the spot and we both knew it, and he wasn't the kind to cry.

I was in his office at nine. By eleven, it was all over and I was on my way home.

I got into Stoneville about dusk, stopped at the show, and ran up to the booth. Hap wasn't there. Jimmie Nedry was running the machines.

"How's it going, Jimmie?" I said. "Giving Mr. Chance a relief?"

"I guess so," he said, not looking at me.

"How soon will he be back, do you know?"

"He ain't coming back," Jimmie said. "He's taking the night off."

"Oh," I said. "Well, I appreciate your working for him, Jimmie."

"Don't mention it."

He got kind of red in the face and moved over between the projectors. I could understand his being embarrassed. Unless he was a lot dumber than I thought he was, he probably knew that I knew what he'd been up to.

I told him good night, just like we were the best pals in the world, and drove over to Hap's hotel. He wasn't there, either. I went on home.

There was a big new black coupé standing in the yard. Hap's, of course. I was plenty glad I'd swung that deal with Panzer. Hap had finished waiting.

He was flopped down on the living-room lounge, a glass and a bottle of whisky at his side; and he had his shoes up on one of Elizabeth's crocheted pillows. The ash tray was full and running over. There was a big circle of ashes and butts on the carpet.

I looked at the mess, and then looked at him. He sat up slowly, grinning.

"Well, laddie," he said. "I get the impression that you've pulled a plum from the pudding—or, shall we say, a phoenix from the fire? Have a drink and tell me about it."

I forced a smile. "Sure, Hap. Where's Carol?"

"In her chambers, I believe. She doesn't seem to be frightfully keen for my company."

"I wonder why?" I said.

I went into the kitchen and brought back a glass and an old newspaper. I spread the paper under the ash tray and set the bottle on it after I'd poured our drinks.

"Clever," Hap nodded. "Too bad you're not married. But give me the news, laddie, I'm all ears."

"You want it right from the beginning?"

"Oh, absolutely."

"Well, right from the start," I said, "I heard that Sol wanted my lot. As soon as I learned that he was moving in, I heard that he was going to take me over. At the exchanges. From you. Everywhere I went. Then, yesterday, just to clinch matters, he drove out here to see me and offered five grand for the lot. He told me he'd give me five to clear out at the end of the season, or I could be stubborn and he'd run me out."

I paused to sip my drink. Hap began to frown.

"He can do it, laddie. Little Sol can take your shirt and charge you interest for wearing it."

"Sure he could."

"So this is the old build-up, eh? The easy letdown. All you've got is a measly five grand."

"Nothing like it," I said. "I didn't sell. Sol doesn't want my lot."

"You said he offered you five yards for it?"

"That's right."

"But he doesn't want it?"

"Of course, he doesn't."

Chance leaned back on the lounge again. He tapped his forehead. "Feeble, laddie. Humor me."

"What would Panzer want with my lot?"

"What would he want with it? Well, fantastic as the idea seems I suppose he'd erect a house on it. There's nothing like the site of an old show for a new one. People are used to the location, and—"

"And," I said, "it's one hundred and three feet from the sidewalk to the alley. No matter how you work it, you can't get much more than a ninety-foot shot from the projection booth to the screen."

Hap blinked. "Lord lummie!" he whispered. "Comes the dawn— But wait a minute! Maybe he intends to pitch his floor in reverse and put the projectors below the screen."

"That still wouldn't give him enough room. Not for a million bucks' worth of house. A million that's got to look like two million."

"But, laddie"—Hap waved his hands—"it's fantastic!"

"Call it anything you want, that's the way it is. There's width and to spare, but not depth. You see how it was, Hap? Sol was using the old magician's trick of misdirection. When I was told that he wanted my lot, over and over, I and everyone else assumed that he did. It never occurred to me to question the fact. Or if I had any idea that it was a little screwy, I brushed it aside. Sol knew what he was doing. He had to know.

"But he got a little too anxious. Too anxious in one way and not enough in another. When he thought that I was convinced, when he believed I was ready to take the five grand, he agreed to let the deal hang fire. I knew, then, that he didn't want my lot. He was misdirecting me. He was doing it because he didn't have the lot sewed up that he did want."

"Careless. I can't believe it of Sol."

"Careless, nothing. Where would he be most likely to tip his hand that he was coming into Stoneville? Why, when he bought his lot. So he was saving that until the last, until he was ready to jump."

"I still say it was careless. Suppose someone jumped in ahead of him—like, I gather, you've done?"

"No one could. What he wanted was the Bower lot, and I had the place leased. I was playing shutout with it. As soon as I went broke, of course, I'd give up my lease and Sol could buy."

Hap shook his head. "Marvelous, laddie. Positively brilliant. And that's the only place in town that Sol could move in on?"

"The only one. That's the only block without an alley; the lots run straight on through. The Bower lot is kind of bottle-shaped. It squares off and spreads out after a few feet."

"And there's no other lot in that block?"

"Two—but the bank and the hotel are sitting on them."

"Terrific! One more question, old bean. How did you happen to acquire this juicy bit of real estate?"

"You know, Hap. I traded something for it that's going to be worthless."

"Uh-hah, your show. That's what I supposed. But there's one little point I'm not quite clear on. Our friend Taylor doesn't know that your house is going to be worthless. He regards it as a little gold mine. Why wasn't he suspicious when you swapped it for his prize white elephant?"

I'd stepped into one again; he knew now that I was walking a pretty ragged rope.

He laughed softly.

"This is much better than I thought, laddie—or worse. Y'know, I think I'll raise my sights on you. I really think I shall."

"What's the Taylor deal got to do with you?" I said. "You don't know anything, Hap."

"Haven't I said so all along? I know enough to sound the alarm. The firemen, speaking metaphorically, will do the rest." He tapped a yawn back with his hand. "Odd how this subject of fires keeps cropping up, isn't it?"

"What do you want?"

"Well, what kind of holdup are you pulling on little Solly? Honor bright, now. I'd be very hurt to catch you in a falsehood."

"I've got a check for fifty grand in my pocket."

"Uh-hah. A very neat evasion. Perhaps I'd better ask Sol about it and explain my interest in the matter."

"I get a hundred and fifty more," I said, "when he moves in."

"You see?" Hap shrugged. "You can tell the truth when you have to." He sat up and reached for the whisky bottle. "Shall we drink on it—partner?"

"Yeah," I said.

"Partner?"

"Partner," I said.

He poured us a drink and we touched glasses; and I couldn't help thinking how nice it would be to drop a little arsenic in his. Then, I saw a shadow in the hall and I knew Carol was listening, and I thought—Well, never mind. Sometimes you get an idea in your head, and it's pretty hard to get it out.

Hap swished the liquor around in his glass, studying me. "Y'know," he said, "you're really a very lucky man, Joe."

"Sure," I said. "Sure, I am."

"Oh, but you are. If I hadn't become interested in the success of your little plan—which necessarily involves your own safety—I probably would have stood aside and let Fate take her course with you. A very unpleasant course."

"Now what?" I said. "What are you trying to pull now?"

"Take yourself back to the morn of the tragedy, old man. You stop by the show and visit the projection booth, and, lo and behold, you discover that your supply of photoelectric cells is exhausted. It comes as a complete surprise to you. You hadn't planned on going to the city, but now you must. *Ergo,* you provide yourself with an alibi for being out of town."

"Well?"

"But you had your suitcase in your car. Jimmie Nedry saw it when he passed by on his way to work. So you must have planned on going to the city before you ever noticed the alleged absence of those cells."

"So what?" I said. "Maybe I was—"

"—taking some clothes to the cleaners? Not good enough, laddie. That could be checked on. And that isn't the clincher, at any rate. It wasn't the first time you'd hopped Jimmie about missing equipment; and he'd taken certain precautions. He's ready to swear that the cells you supposedly bought in town bore the same serial numbers as those that were missing from the show. In other words, old chap, your alibi is a phony."

"He—he told you all this?"

"Mmm. Got quite fond of me, did Nedry. And in the morning, when Blair swings his transfer, he's going to tell him."

He grinned at me over his glass, and I began to see red. What the hell! This was my deal. I'd taken the risk and done all the thinking, and here was another guy with his hand out!

"Let the little bastard talk," I said. "Let him go to hell. He's lying! He got the numbers of those cells wrong. He—"

"Huh-ah. But even if he had it wouldn't make any difference. You still couldn't afford to have him tell that story."

"He can tell anything he pleases! By God, I'm—"

Hap's hand shot out. He caught his fingers in my collar and jerked and twisted.

For a minute I thought my neck was broken.

"That's how a rope feels, laddie. Just a little like that. But don't fret. If you crumb this deal, I'll settle with you myself."

My throat felt like I'd swallowed a cantaloupe. "How—h-how much do you think—"

"Nothing. Not a red."

"Nothing?"

"No money. It wouldn't do any good. Your projectionist has one of the most alarming cases of honesty I've ever seen. He's even conscience-stricken at having used his information to pry a better job out of Blair."

"But he hasn't told him yet?"

"He hasn't. And he won't."

"I see," I said. And he nodded and looked at his wrist watch.

"Well, I really must be shoving along. I told them at the hotel that I'd be checking out tonight. Told several people, in fact. Must be getting back to the city."

"I hate to see you leave," I said.

"It's trying, isn't it? But the best of friends, you know, and all that rot— Oh yes—"

"Yeah?"

"It's terribly lonely when friend Nedry gets off work. Been thinking it might be awfully awkward for you if he should be slugged by footpads or some such thing. Perhaps you'd best be at home here around eleven-thirty. Miss Farmer can alibi for you."

"Okay, Hap," I said.

"On second thought, I incline to the belief that some doubt might be cast on the Farmer veracity. Call your telephone operator at eleven-thirty. Ask her the time. They still give it here, don't they?"

"Yes."

"Cheerio, then."

"Cheer—so long," I said.

26

There was a chocolate cake in the refrigerator and part of a baked ham. But I passed them up and opened a can of soup. I wasn't particularly hungry, and I'd been eating too much recently. Just this morning I'd noticed that I was getting a little paunchy.

I heard Carol come through the door, and I could feel her standing behind me. I went on eating and pretty soon she walked around into my line of vision. And it was all I could do not to burst out laughing.

She had a new kind of hairdo, and a plain black dress, and she was trying to stick her nose in the air and hold her chin down at the same time. Sure, Elizabeth. Or Carol's idea of Elizabeth.

I ducked my head over my soup.

"You look mighty pretty, Carol," I said, as soon as I could say anything.

"Do you like me better this way?"

I wasn't sure of the answer to that one. "You always look good to me. How about some soup?"

"I've already ate—eaten."

"Coffee?"

"No. You go ahead."

I went ahead, taking my time about it, doing some thinking. This was the second or third time she'd listened in on my conversations. She was nervous and scared, of course, but, hell, I was a little uneasy myself, and I didn't pop out at her every time she opened a door.

I wondered if it was always going to be like this. I wondered if I could never go any place or do anything without having her breathing down my neck.

Without worrying about her getting worried.

I shoved my plate back and lighted a cigarette. "I guess you know," I said, "that there's been some trouble."

She nodded. "Yes. I know *now.*"

"I'm glad you heard," I said. "I intended to tell you as soon as I could see my way out. Didn't want to worry you unless I had to."

"You—you weren't afraid to tell me, Joe?"

"Now, why do you say a thing like that?"

"I—I couldn't stand it if you were afraid of me, Joe! I know how you feel—how you got to feel. I'm different, now! When you kill someone it changes you. But—"

"I was afraid," I said, "but not that way. You'd stuck your neck out. It looked like it might not get you anything. You might have thought that we—I—had known it wouldn't get you anything. That I'd put you on a spot, and was going to walk off and leave you."

"And try to go to Elizabeth?" she snapped.

"You see?" I said. "Now get that idea out of your head, Carol. I had Elizabeth and I didn't want her. She had me, and she didn't want me. I figure she brought you here with the idea that I'd fall for you."

"Oh, no, she didn't!"

"She had some reason for doing it, and it sure wasn't charity."

"She wanted me around to make herself look good!

I'm a woman myself and I know. That's why I hated her so much! Don't you suppose if she'd wanted to get rid of you she'd have got someone that didn't look like—like—"

"Carol," I said, and I got up and put my arm around her and gave her a hug.

The dame *was* nuts if she thought that about Elizabeth. Elizabeth didn't need anyone around to make her look good.

"Well, it's the truth," Carol said.

"No, it's not," I said, leading her into the living-room. "And you're getting yourself all upset over nothing. All that matters is that we'll be in the clear after tonight, and we'll have plenty of money. Let's not spoil it."

"Promise you won't try to see her, Joe."

"Of course, I won't," I said. "Do you think I'd run a risk like that?"

"You'll give me her—the money and let me send it to her?"

"I told you I would. Now forget it."

She wiped her eyes and smiled, sort of trembly; and I fixed us a drink. I thought for a minute the arguments and explanations were over, but of course they weren't.

I was beginning to see that they weren't ever going to be over. I wondered how Elizabeth felt about it all now.

"How long will it be before everything is settled, Joe?"

"Two or three months, anyway."

"Can I stay here until—"

"No," I said. "You know you can't, Carol."

"Just until that insurance man leaves, Joe! Just let me stay that long. He—he scares me. I don't want to be away from you as long as he's around."

"Well," I said, "we'll see."

I meant to get her out of the house in the next day or two if I had to pitch her out a window.

Rain began to patter on the roof. It started in easy, and got harder and harder. Inside of a half hour it was a regular downpour. There was a hell of a crash of lightning somewhere near by, and Carol shuddered and snuggled close to me. I reached back to the wall and turned on the furnace.

"Joe."

"Yeah," I said.

"It's kind of nice being this way, ain't—isn't it? Being able to do just what we please around the house."

"I'll say."

"Elizabeth would say it was too early for the furnace."

"Yeah, she sure would." It sounded pretty half-hearted, so I had to say something else. "If you wanted to see someone that was really tight you should have seen her old lady. We cleaned out her room after she died, and she had darned near a whole closet full of dry bread—just scraps, you know."

Carol snickered. "She must have been crazy."

"I guess she was along toward the last. You could hardly blame her, though, with a husband that spent all his life writing a history of the county."

"What'd he do that for?"

"God knows," I said.

Carol snuggled closer. The room began to get warm. The wind rose and fell, throwing the rain against the roof in long steady swishes; and she seemed to breathe in time with it.

My knees began to ache from her weight, but I

didn't move. I didn't want to talk any more about Elizabeth or her folks or anything. Everything was all right now. I'd told her about a hundred times that I loved her and didn't love Elizabeth. A man can't spend his life hashing over the past.

I dozed for a few minutes, what seemed like a few minutes. When I woke up, the clock had just finished striking.

I jerked out my watch. Eleven-thirty. I shoved Carol off of me, waking her up, and stumbled out to the hall. My legs had gone to sleep and I could hardly walk.

The phone rang just as I was gripping the receiver. I answered it automatically.

"Joe?"

"Yes."

"I've got to talk with you, Joe. How soon can you come down?"

"Why," I said, "what's wrong?"

"I'm at my office. You'll be right down?"

"Well— It's kind of a bad night."

No answer.

"Well, sure," I said. "I'll be right down."

I hung up.

Carol was still sitting on the lounge, her face whiter than anything I ever hope or want to see. Her lips moved, but no sound came out of them.

"Web Clay," I said; and, as if she didn't know: "Our county attorney."

27

She swallowed a couple of times and finally found her voice.

"W-What does he want?"

"I don't know."

"Mr. Chance?"

"Goddamit," I said. "I told you I didn't know!"

Hap wasn't supposed to call; he was going right on into the city. But I didn't think it could be about him. Hap was too smooth an operator to be taken in by any of the Stoneville clowns. If there'd been a chance of being caught he wouldn't have taken it.

But even if they had got him, what could he say? What could Jimmie Nedry say, for that matter? Enough to start the ball rolling, sure, but the ball hadn't had time to roll yet. Even Web Clay wasn't dumb enough to tip his hand to me until he had a lot more to go on than he would have.

I went over to the hall tree and took down my hat and coat. And ...

And she didn't say anything and I didn't hear her move. But her hand went past mine and grabbed her coat.

I jumped, startled. Before I knew what I was doing, I whirled and slammed her against the wall. It hurt her. It hurt and I was damned glad of it.

She bounced forward, trying to dodge around me; and I caught her by the wrists and we struggled. And then we stopped, posed like a couple of wrestlers in a picture. Ashamed. Scared stiff.

"Sorry if I hurt you, baby," I said. "You kind of startled me."

"It's all right, Joe." She tried to smile back at me. "I just want to go with you."

"You know you can't. How would it look, Carol?"

"I've got to, Joe!"

"You can't!"

"No one knows there's anything between—"

"You're damned right they don't," I said, "and they're not going to, either. What would you be doing up at this time of night? Why would you be traipsing along with me?"

"You don't understand, Joe. I—I—"

"I understand all right," I said. "You're afraid I'll spill something. You want to get in on the ground floor when the talking starts."

It was a bad break but I couldn't hold it back. I'd held myself in as long as I could. Anyway, she might as well know that I was onto her. We knew where we stood now.

"Do—do you really think that, Joe?"

"What do you expect me to think? You're certainly not worried about me chasing off after Elizabeth."

"No. I'm not worried about that."

"Spit it out, then, if you've got anything to say."

"You'd better go on, Joe."

"You'll stay here?"

"Where else would I go? Yes, I'll stay here."

I shrugged on my coat and pushed past her. She spoke again, just as I was opening the door.

"Joe—"

"Now what?"

"I just wanted to tell you, Joe. Everything's going to be all right. You don't have anything to be afraid of."

"Not any more than you have," I said. "Not as much. Don't forget it."

I got the car started, and went slipping and skidding down the lane to the highway. At the intersection I jerked the wheel toward the right, toward town. I had to jerk it. Something had almost made me turn the other way.

People in Stoneville go to bed pretty early, even when there isn't a storm to keep them off the streets. I toured around a dozen blocks without passing anyone or without seeing any lights except those in the courthouse. There were a few cars parked out, but none of them was Hap's. I began to breathe easier. He must have done the job and got away.

There was just one way to make sure, of course. That was to drive by Jimmie Nedry's house and see if he was there. But I didn't have any reason for doing that, any excuse I mean, and there wasn't time.

It was almost a half hour, now, since Web had called me. Regardless of what had happened, he'd start wondering if I didn't show up soon.

I drove back to the courthouse, parked, and ran up the walk to the building. I went up the stairs and down the hall, not hurrying but not taking my time, either, just businesslike. I put the right kind of expression on my face—puzzled and a little put out—and then I opened Web's door and went in.

Web was sitting behind his desk, looking about as uncomfortable as I felt. Sheriff Rufe Waters was standing, leaning against the wall. He acted like he didn't want any part of what was going on.

I sat down in front of Web, slapped the rain from my hat, and waited. He made a job of clearing his throat.

"Well, Joe," he said at last. "I suppose you're wondering why I asked you to come down here."

"You can't blame me for that," I said.

Rufe laughed and muttered something under his breath, and Web gave him an angry look.

"Rufe thinks I'm playing the fool," he said. "But I'm running this office, and I've got to do what I think is best. I wouldn't have had you come down here, Joe, if I hadn't figured I had to."

"So?" I said.

"Well, I just wanted to know, Joe—I wondered if you thought, perhaps—"

Rufe Waters laughed again.

"I'll tell you, Joe. He thinks it wasn't Mrs. Wilmot that got killed in the fire."

28

I tried to keep from jumping. Then I remembered that
I should, that anyone would be startled by a statement
of that kind; and I gave a good healthy start.

I leaned forward, frowning, interested.

"Web must have some reason for thinking that," I
said. "What is it, Web?"

He wiped his face, relieved that I wasn't sore. "Has
Appleton said anything to you about a woman he was
looking for? A woman that came out here on the day of
the fire and disappeared?"

"Why, yes," I said, "I believe he did make some
mention of it."

"Well, that's it. He prowled the town from one end
to the other looking for her, and then he called us in
and we checked with everyone that hires household
help. Everyone but you, and, of course, Elizabeth."

"Yes," I said. "Go on, Web."

"Well, Joe, we figure—Appleton and I figure—that
that woman must have gone to your place."

"She didn't," I said. "Elizabeth didn't say anything
about hiring anyone."

"But that doesn't mean she didn't do it!" Web
laughed apologetically. "No offense. I just mean she
wouldn't have been a Barclay if she hadn't been a wee
bit highhanded. All the Barclays were."

"You're right about that," I said. "But—"

"You were in the city, Joe. You didn't go home after you left in the morning. So the woman could have been there, and you wouldn't have known a thing about it."

I shook my head, stalling; waiting to be convinced. I could see where the conversation was leading, but there wasn't anything to do but follow it. It was a crazy way for things to turn out, to be tripped up by a dame that didn't belong in the plot at all. But there it was.

And I couldn't help Carol. All I could do was save myself.

"I don't think Elizabeth would have done that," I said. "But give me the rest of it."

"Here's the way we see it," said Web. "Mrs. Wilmot put an ad in one of the city papers and hired this woman. She hired her, and the Farmer girl didn't know about it until Mrs. Wilmot picked her up that night in Wheat City. Probably Elizabeth was a little bit curt, and Carol got sore. You couldn't blame her much. Here she was coming back from a vacation, with all her money spent more'n likely, and she finds herself out of a job.

"It's thirty miles from here to Wheat City. We figure that somewhere between here and there, Elizabeth was killed and her body hid. We figure that Carol drove on home by herself, killed the other woman to keep from giving her play away, and then put her in the garage and set it on fire."

"I—I can't believe that Carol would do anything like that, Web."

"Oh, she could have." Rufe Waters spoke up. "All them Farmers are a dead-hard lot. I wouldn't put a killin' or two past any member of that family. But the rest of it's all bunk. I mean about this other woman, and all."

Web glared at him. "What's bunk about it? It all fits in, don't it?"

"I ain't going to argue," said Rufe. "I'll go along with you so far as to say that the girl might have had an argument with Mrs. Wilmot and killed her, but that's as far as I will go."

"I can't believe it," I said again. "Carol and Elizabeth got along fine—at least, while I was around."

"Well," drawled Web, "what getting-along is to a man isn't the same as it is to a woman. A man doesn't really know when womenfolks are at outs and when they're not."

"But if Elizabeth hadn't wanted her around—"

"—she'd have fired her," said Web. "And I'm claiming that's just what she did do! She went right ahead without asking or telling anyone and canned her."

Rufe scratched his head thoughtfully. Web had made a point with him.

"It's a little too pat," I said. "Carol had been with us for almost a year. If Elizabeth had wanted to fire her, it looks like she'd have done it long ago."

"Maybe the trouble just came up lately. Maybe Elizabeth couldn't find anyone to take her place. Maybe she was waiting until Carol was out of town. That's common sense, isn't it?"

"Well," I hesitated, "it sounds reasonable."

"I tell you, Joe; it just had to be something like that. The more you think about, the more you see I'm right. I'm not saying that the girl just hauled off and deliberately started killing. Probably it was kind of an accident to begin with. She was mad. She flung out at

Elizabeth and killed her before she knew what she was doing. Then she had to go on and do the rest to protect herself."

He stared at me, waiting, and I nodded my head a couple of times. "I don't know, Web. The way you put it—"

"It's a cinch that fire didn't start itself," said Rufe Waters.

"No, it didn't," said Web. "The girl had to do it, Joe. She was the only one that could have."

I could have said, "How can you be so damned sure that the woman stayed here? How do you know she's not in some other burg right now, throwing herself a whing-ding?"

But what I said was, "Maybe you're right."

"It's not just my idea," Web went on. "This insurance fellow, Appleton, really thought of it. Didn't he ask you anything about how things stood between Carol and Mrs. Wilmot?"

"Yes, he did."

"Well, he—we hadn't really started putting two and two together, then. We thought it was just a matter of a little work to turn this missing woman up. When we couldn't find her he started putting two and two together, and we figured it like I just told you. He heard from his company tonight, and they think he's on the right track. They're willing to back him up in anything he does. That's why I got you down here."

"I see," I said.

"Appleton's going to ask that the bod— that the remains be exhumed and examined in the morning. He's going to demand a *real* post mortem. If it don't show it was Elizabeth that was killed in the fire, he's going to put a murder charge against Carol Farmer. I don't like to have him running things on me like that. I figure if there's any murders to be solved we people here in the county ought to solve 'em ourselves."

"Especially with election coming up," nodded Rufe.

"That's got nothing to do with it!" Web glared at him. "Now, here's what I thought we'd better do, Joe. There's no use in Rufe or me trying to talk to that girl. She'd just freeze up on us, like the rest of that ornery Farmer gang. So I want you to talk to her. Tell her—"

"Me talk to her?" I said.

"Yes, you, Joe."

"Well, gosh," I said. "I—"

"You know how to gentle people along, get on the best side of 'em. You can get her to talk when no one else could get to first base. You know. Sympathize with her, but show her she hasn't got a chance to beat the case. I know it's asking a lot, but—"

"I don't think it is." I looked from Web to Rufe, jutting my jaw out. "If things are like you think they are, it's my duty to help to get to the bottom of 'em!"

"I knew you'd see it that way, Joe."

"The only reason I'd hesitate at all is because of the possibility that I might gum things up. If the girl is guilty, I want to be sure she pays the penalty. What'll I do if she tries to skip out, or—"

"Just a minute," said Rufe.

He crossed the room, opened the connecting door to his offices, and went inside. He came back with a Colt automatic in his hand. He twirled it, caught it by the barrel, and handed it to me butt first.

"You take that, Joe."

"Well," I said, shying away. "I don't know as *that's* necessary."

"Take it, Joe," said Web. "That girl may have a gun herself for all you or we know. She might come at you with a knife. She might try to knock you out with a

club and make a run for it. You can't take any
chances. You take the gun, and if you have to use it,
don't hesitate."

I held back a few minutes longer. But finally they
talked me into taking it.

29

Driving home in the rain, with my guts kind of knotting and unknotting, I thought about Elizabeth and how goddam unfair it was that I had to do all the dirty work on a deal she'd really started.

I hadn't hired Carol. I never would have brought her into the house. Maybe I wasn't too satisfied with married life, but it never occurred to me to do anything about it. It was Elizabeth who had brought her in. It was just one more stupid thing she'd done that I had to be the fall guy for.

About a year after she'd had her miscarriage I went home one afternoon and some dame was in the living-room with Elizabeth. I stuck my head in the door to say hello, and she and this woman both looked kind of embarrassed. And then Elizabeth laughed and told me to come in.

"This is Mrs. Fahrney, Joe," she said. "Mrs. Fahrney is connected with the children's protective society."

"Oh?" I said, wondering if she had a kick on some of the shows I'd been playing. "That must be very interesting work."

"Well—it is," said the dame, glancing at Elizabeth.

And Elizabeth laughed again.

"We may as well tell him," she said. "He'll have to sign the papers, anyway."

"The papers?" I said.

"I was keeping it for a surprise, dear. We're going to have a son. The sweetest little boy baby you ever—"

"Wait a minute," I said. "You mean you want to adopt someone else's kid?"

"Not someone else's, Joe. Ours. Perhaps I should have told you sooner, but—"

"I guess you should have, too," I said. "I guess you might have saved this lady a trip out here if you had. Any time I have any kids of my own I guarantee I'll feed 'em and take care of 'em and do everything else I'm supposed to. But I'm not spending my dough and my time on other people's brats. I don't want any part of 'em."

Elizabeth sat biting her lip, looking down at the floor. This woman got up and walked over to her.

"I'm sorry, Mrs. Wilmot," she said. "I'll run along now."

"Oh, wait a minute," I said. "I didn't mean all that. If she wants to adopt this—boy, it's all right with me."

"But it isn't all right with me," she said, looking straight through me. "Good-by, Mrs. Wilmot."

And she sailed out the door without giving me a chance to reason with her.

I tried to explain to Elizabeth how I felt. A kid is always a hell of a big expense and we just couldn't spare the dough from the show. And, anyway, how could you tell what you were getting into when you take a kid out of an orphans' home?

All Elizabeth would say was, "I understand," and she didn't understand at all.

Well, no one can say I'm not human, and I was kind of ashamed of the way I'd acted. I suppose she did get lonesome around the place by herself, and when she got a cat I didn't say a word. I don't like cats. They demand too much attention. If you're trying to read or eat or no matter what you're trying to do a cat will butt right in on you. Short of killing them, there's no way of keeping them from rubbing against your legs or jumping into your lap or just bothering you in general.

I didn't say a word, though. When it got to where it bothered me too much I'd just go to my room and lock the door.

I guess it finally got on Elizabeth's nerves, too, because she gave it away to someone. I never asked who and she didn't say. I was just satisfied that it was gone.

About six months later she bought a dog—a tan-and-white collie pup. And I didn't say anything about that, either, but I never knew a minute's comfort at home until she got rid of it. I can't stand dogs. I mean, I can't. And if you'd been on the bum as much as I have, you'd know why.

Well, so that brings us up to Carol. And I know what you're thinking—it's what I thought at first—but it's not the case. She didn't take Carol as a substitute for the cat or dog. She didn't treat her half as good as she'd treated either one of them.

I've already told you how she didn't even give her a decent feed the first night she was there. That's just a sample of the way she acted toward her. And it didn't get me anywhere when I jumped her about it.

"Really, Joe, you amaze me," she said, sort of smiling down her nose. "How can you possibly be interested in the welfare of a girl like that? I'm already willing to admit it was a mistake to bring her here."

"Well, she's here," I said, "and she's going to stay. And we're going to treat her decent, too."

"Are we?"

"All right, don't, then," I said. "But if you won't do anything for her yourself, don't stand in my way."

"I won't," she said, still smiling. "That's a promise. I won't stand in your way at all." And that was the way it ended.

All that was ever done for Carol was done by me. I hadn't lied to Appleton about that. But it was Elizabeth that brought her into the house in the first place. I don't know why, unless it was just another one of her ways of getting my goat, and I don't know that it matters.

All I know is that Carol coming there is what started all the trouble, and that it was left to me to clean it up.

There was one thing that still puzzled me and always had—the money. The way Elizabeth had argued about a split. The way she'd kept telling me I'd be sorry if I tried to get out of sending her the insurance dough.

The people who really care about money are those who lack something without it, and Elizabeth had always felt just as complete and respectable and important without a dollar as she had with a pocketful. She'd been saving and thrifty, sure, but that was more habit than anything else. She'd proved a hundred times over that money didn't mean a thing to her.

When she'd first begun to make an issue of it I thought she was just trying to put a spoke in my wheel, to make it harder to settle the problem between her and Carol and me. And right up until the last, I guess, I was expecting her to say, "All right, have your Carol and everything else. I'd scrub floors before I'd take a penny from you."

That would have been Elizabeth's way of doing things, and maybe I would have taken her up on it and maybe I wouldn't have. The point is that she did just the opposite—something that just didn't fit in with her character. And now when it mattered least of all, I couldn't get it out of my mind.

I remembered how insistent Carol had been on sending Elizabeth the money herself, and the answer to that one popped into my head and made me shiver. She hadn't intended sending it. She'd have burned it up first. She hated her enough to do that, to risk getting us all in trouble just to take one final punch at Elizabeth.

It had to be the answer, because I never wrote even a business letter if I could get out of it and I sure wouldn't have written Elizabeth after we were all washed up. It was a standing joke around the house, my not writing to anyone. At least it had been a joke back in the beginning, back during the first year that Elizabeth and I were married.

We were awfully cramped for dough that year. We had good prospects and I knew we'd pull out in the long run, but I was trying to do too many things at once and we ran short. It got so bad that I even considered closing down for a while and going back to driving film truck. But right at the time when things looked darkest this old uncle of Elizabeth's died back East, and everything was jake. He left her twenty-five hundred dollars, enough to clear up the mortgage on the Barclay home with a thousand left over.

Well, I took her down to the train when she started back to collect, and while we were waiting on the platform she asked me to send her a dollar.

"Send you a dollar?" I laughed. "What's the idea? Here, I'll give you—"

"No, I want you to send it to me, Joe. I know that's the only way I'll hear from you."

"Oh, now," I said. "I don't think I'm that bad. I'll drop you a card."

"Oh, but you are that bad," she said. "Send me the dollar or you'll be sorry when I come back."

She was kidding, you know, like newly married people will. But I thought if it meant that much to her I'd play along. And that was the cause of two of the worst weeks I've ever spent in my life.

I am careful about money; a businessman has got to be. I'd double-checked the hotel address where Elizabeth was supposed to be staying, and I put a five-day return on the envelope when I mailed it. And then, through some kind of mix-up, it came back to me, and the envelope was stamped *Not known here.*

Scared? Worried? Brother!

I didn't know where else to write. I knew she was supposed to be at the address I had. And, of course, she thought I'd broken my promise so she didn't write me, either. She finally broke down and sent me a wire, and I sent her one, and—and that was the end of it.

But until I heard from her I was imagining all sorts of things. I'd about halfway decided that she must be dead ...

30

I used to know a drunk years ago, a booker at one of the film exchanges in the city. He was one of those God-awful, noisy, messy drunks; the worst of the worst kind. And do you know something? That guy couldn't stand the sight of another drunk. It wasn't any pretense. He actually hated 'em. He'd walk six blocks to keep from passing one on the street.

I was thinking about him, and wondering why I was thinking about him, as I turned into the lane toward home. Then, as I drove into the yard, another funny thing popped into my mind—the tag line on an old joke. *It's not the original cost but the upkeep.*

There it is. Make anything you want to out of it.

After I'd shut off the motor I sat in the car for a moment, pulling myself together; thinking—trying to think—what a hell of a mess Carol had got me into by going to work for us. Then, I rubbed the gun in my pocket, wiped the sweat off my hand, and got out.

I went up the steps.

I crossed the porch and opened the door.

As far as I could see, there from the hall, everything was just like I had left it. The shades were drawn. The furnace was still ticking away, throwing out warm waves of heat. The lights were ...

"Carol," I called. "Carol!"

And every light in the place went out.

I stood where I was, paralyzed; too shocked to move. And the air from the furnace didn't seem warm any more. It got colder and colder. It brushed against my face like the draft from an icebox. Somehow I got my foot behind me and kicked the door shut. As an afterthought, I turned the key in the lock and put it in my pocket.

I called her one more time. "Carol!"

There wasn't any answer.

It wasn't the storm, then. She'd pulled the switch. She'd done it without even waiting to see what Web had wanted, or what I was going to do about it. And she'd been nagging me about not trusting her!

I was sore and relieved at the same time. It made things easier.

I started to strike a match, but caught myself. She'd see me first; and she hadn't turned out those lights for the fun of it. She was sure I'd put her on the spot. Or, maybe, she'd guessed that I could never feel safe as long as she was alive. Anyway, she was playing for keeps.

I don't know whether I've described the layout of our house or not. There's a hall extending from the front door to the kitchen. On the left, as you go in, is the living-room. The dining-room is across from it, on the right.

I went down the hall on tiptoe to the living-room, and eased the drapes apart. My eyes were getting used to the dark, and I could see a little. Not much, but a little. The outlines of the furniture; shadowy blotches on the wall where pictures hung.

The living-room looked empty, and I decided it must be. The master light switch was in the kitchen. She hadn't had time to move far from it.

I tried to figure out which way she'd go. Up the hall toward me, or through the door into the dining-room? Or would she still be there in the kitchen?

I started down the hall. And stopped.

A door had creaked. The door connecting the dining-room and kitchen. She was coming around that way. Getting behind me.

I pivoted and crept back to the dining-room. I slid through the portiers, holding my breath.

The door creaked again as it was opened wider. Now I could see a black oblong as it was opened all the way.

I could see a shadow, a crouched blur upon the black.

I touched the trigger of the automatic.

The explosion was almost deafening, but I heard her scamper back into the kitchen. I heard one of the chairs go over. I eased forward again, not seeing too well because of the flash of light from the shot. At the door into the kitchen I dropped down on my hands and knees and started to crawl across the threshold.

It was a minute or two before I saw her, her shadow against the far wall. I waited until I was sure, until I saw it edging toward the spot where the hall door would be. Then, slowly, I began rising to my feet.

I was too slow for her. In a split second the door banged open. Crashed shut.

I stood up, panting, sweat pouring from my face. I felt my way along the wall to the switch box.

The cover was open, as I'd known it would be, and the switch was pulled. I pushed it back into place, blinking my eyes as the lights went on. I locked the back door and put the key in my pocket. I waited, looking upward.

Listening.

At last I heard it. The squeak of a bedspring. I started to tiptoe out of the kitchen, then stopped again. She'd have to come out of her room. It wouldn't look right to break the door down.

I began to whistle to myself, as I thought it over. And then I started to whistle louder, loud enough for her to hear me and just as if I didn't have a care in the world.

I tramped up the stairs, and knocked on the door of her bedroom.

"Carol!" I called. "Are you asleep?"

There was no answer, but the bed creaked again. In my mind I could see her sitting there, huddled as far back as she could get. Staring at the door.

I let out an embarrassed laugh. "Did you hear all that racket I was making? The light switch dropped down and shut off the current. I thought there was a prowler in the house." I laughed again. "Guess I'd be shooting yet if my gun hadn't jammed."

I *could* own a gun. She couldn't be sure that I didn't.

I heard—I thought I heard—a faint sigh of relief. A scared, doubtful sigh.

"Get dressed, Carol. We've got to get out of here. Right away, tonight."

There wasn't any kind of sound this time; nothing I could identify. But she seemed to be asking a question.

"Do you hear me, Carol?" I knocked again. "We've got to beat it. They've found out about the woman you hired. They haven't got the straight of things, but they know enough. They're going to open the grave in the morning. As soon as they find out it wasn't Elizabeth, we'll be sunk. They'll run Elizabeth down, and she'll squawk, to save her own neck. The whole thing will be pinned on us." I banged harder on the door.

"Come on! We can be a long ways from here by daylight. Open the door and I'll help you pack!"

She didn't answer. It dawned on me that she probably couldn't. She was too frightened, too scared of what her voice might tell me.

But she had got up. She was standing. And now she was coming to the door.

Afraid, yes. Scared as hell. But more scared not to.

I raised and leveled the gun. My hand was shaking, and I gripped my wrist with my other hand and steadied it.

The key grated and clicked in the lock. The doorknob turned.

Then the door flew open, and just as it did I squeezed the trigger.

There was one long, stuttering explosion. And then it was all over.

And through the smoke I saw Appleton grinning at me.

31

"Thanks a lot. I think that establishes an intention to kill, even though you were shooting blanks." His grin broadened, seeming to contract his eyes. "Not that we needed it after your interesting revelations. You're a hard man, Joe. We thought you'd give the gal some kind of explanation before you started shooting."

"I—I—" I said. "The sheriff gave me that gun. I—I thought she was going to kill me, and—"

"Oh, come now, Joe." He shook his head. "Who do you think was playing that game of tag with you— trying to get you to open up? Why do you think Waters gave you a gun loaded with blanks? What do you think happened to your buddy, Chance?"

I swallowed. Hard. "You got—Hap?"

"Uh-huh. Caught him right in the act of slugging Jimmie Nedry. He was quite co-operative, but his information wasn't very helpful. He put the finger on you, but it didn't mean anything to us. Not any more than what Andy Taylor had to tell."

"Cut it out!" I laughed in his face. I was caught, but that didn't mean I was a sucker. "If Andy had told you anything—"

"Of course, he did, Joe. Think a minute. What could you possibly offer a man in Taylor's position that would reimburse him for the risk of a long prison sentence? Don't put yourself in his place. It doesn't work. Taylor told us when you offered to cancel the lease on the Bower. Nedry told us about the stunt with the photoelectric cells; Nedry and Blair. But that still didn't give us enough. You could have had a change of heart with Taylor. Nedry and Blair were sore at you."

He paused, one eyebrow raised, and I nodded.

"Go on. Give it all to me."

"You already know it, Joe. Most of it, anyway. I was sure that you'd loved your wife. I knew that if the fire had been set you couldn't have done it since you were out of town. That gave us one, or, rather, two possibilities to work on. If a crime had been committed Carol was involved in it. And if you were really covering up for her—and we couldn't be sure that you were—then you were in on it, too, and—"

His voice trailed off, and he paused again. And it seemed as if he was trying not to look at me.

"Maybe you'd better sit down, Joe."

"What the hell for?" I said. "I can take it. I can hand it out and I can t-take it. You figured that we must have—must have brought in another woman. You made up that story about looking for one to see how I'd take it. That's it, ain't—isn't it? There wasn't any other woman, was there?"

"No, Joe, there wasn't. When I first gave you the yarn I thought it had struck home. But later on, that night in my hotel room, I wasn't sure. In fact, I'd have been willing to bet that you were on the level. If you hadn't made that one-sided swap with Andy Taylor—"

"Jesus!" I laughed. "Jesus Christ! I gave you the cards myself. If I'd just sat tight you'd never have known about—that it wasn't Elizabeth."

He shook his head. "You don't understand, Joe.

Waters and Clay were your friends. They didn't want to tell you something that might hurt your feelings. That was in the beginning. Later on, when this Nedry and Taylor business developed, they agreed to keep quiet. They were safe enough regardless of how the thing turned out. You couldn't blame them for not mentioning a routine measure, particularly since I'd instigated it."

"You're talking a lot," I said. "You're talking a lot and you're not s-saying—you're not saying—"

"Better accept it, Joe. Face it and get it over with."

"I—I don't know what—"

"You must know. Otherwise we'd have arrested you right in the beginning. I don't know why she did it. I don't know why she came back here and walked into the trap she'd helped to set. That's something for you to figure out if you haven't already got it figured. All I can tell you is this, Joe. We identified the body days ago, and"—his voice dropped—"Carol came back from the city alone."

His hand shot out as I staggered. I threw it off.

"Carol— Where is she?"

"Look on the bed, Joe."

He stood aside.

I looked.

The haft of the scissors stood out from her breast like an unclasped pin. That was all I could see of her. The scissors, and her breast arched up to meet it.

"She left a note, Joe. A confession. She was going to take all the blame on herself. I put the screws on her, and she told me she'd talk to the county attorney. I let her come up here to get ready, and—"

He broke off, watching me.

"If she'd told me," I said. "If she'd told me—"

"Yes, Joe? If she'd told you she'd killed the woman you loved?"

I looked from the bed to him. I looked back at the bed. I took a step forward.

"Would it, Joe? Would it have been all right?"

I didn't answer him. I couldn't. I didn't know the answer until I reached the bed. And then I knew, but there weren't any words left in me.

It wasn't the way she looked, but the way I did. Because all I'd ever seen in her was myself, the little of myself that was pitying and compassionate and unselfish or whatever you want to call it. And, now, in the ending, even that little was gone. And all that was left was what I could see here, in her eyes. Dead eyes, turning in slightly.

I shivered and tried to look away.

I thought, *They can't hang me. I'm already dead. I've been dead a long, long time.*

GLOSSARY OF EXHIBITOR TERMS

B.O.
box office (receipts)

DARK
not in operation; a dark house

GRIND-HOUSE
a show which operates 24 hours daily

INDIE
an independent exhibitor or exchange

ONE-SHEET (THREE-SHEET etc.)
posters. Largest dimension is the 24-billboard size

PAPER
advertising matter

PRODUCT
pictures

SOUND HEADS
the part of the projector which picks up the sound from the film. See below.

SOUND TABLE
a now-obsolete device, similar to a phonograph, used in transcribing sound. Dialogue and musical accompaniment of early "talkies" were recorded on discs which were synchronized (perhaps!) with the film by the projectionist. An imperfect and expensive arrangement, it was supplanted by the recording of sound on the film proper and the use of sound heads.

About the Author

James Meyers Thompson was born in Anadarko, Oklahoma, in 1906. He began writing fiction at a very young age, selling his first story to *True Detective* when he was only fourteen. In all, Jim Thompson wrote twenty-nine novels and two screenplays (for the Stanley Kubrick films *The Killing* and *Paths of Glory*). Films based on his novels include: *Coup de Torchon (Pop. 1280), Serie Noire (A Hell of a Woman), The Getaway, The Killer Inside Me, The Grifters,* and *After Dark, My Sweet*. A biography of Jim Thompson will be published by Knopf.